Essex County Council

Many libraries in Essex have
facilities for exhibitions
and meetings —

enquire at your local library
for details

MONSIEUR PAMPLEMOUSSE
ON LOCATION

MONSIEUR PAMPLEMOUSSE ON LOCATION

Michael Bond

HEADLINE

First published in 1992
by HEADLINE BOOK PUBLISHING PLC

10 9 8 7 6 5 4 3 2 1

British Library Cataloguing in Publication Data

Bond, Michael
    Monsieur Pamplemousse on Location
    I. Title
    823.914 [F]

ISBN 0-7472-0673-2

Typeset by
Letterpart Limited, Reigate, Surrey

Printed and bound in Great Britain by
Clays Ltd, St Ives PLC

HEADLINE BOOK PUBLISHING PLC
Headline House
79 Great Titchfield Street
London W1P 7FN

CONTENTS

1
OVERTURE AND BEGINNERS

For Monsieur Pamplemousse it began and ended in the Parc Monceau; that small but immaculately kept oasis of greenery situated in the 8th *arrondissement* of Paris, where uniformed nannies from well-to-do families for-gather every afternoon in order to give the occupants of their *voitures d'enfant* an airing.

Fate had drawn him there in the first place. Fate and Pommes Frites, which more often than not amounted to much the same thing.

The day had started badly. *En route* to the office, he encountered a horrendous traffic jam in the Place de Clichy. An *embouteillage* of the very worst kind. A quick glance to his left as he joined the throng of impatient drivers revealed stationary traffic as far as the eye could see – all the way down the rue de Léningrad.

Without a moment's hesitation, Monsieur Pample-mousse abandoned his normal route and put Plan 'B' into action. After mounting the central reservation for a short distance, he wormed his way with great aplomb in and out of the waiting vehicles and headed westwards along the Boulevard des Batignolles as though that had been his intention all along.

A few minutes later, soon after they reached the Boulevard Courcelles to be exact, he felt a stirring in the back seat of his 2CV as Pommes Frites came to and

1

registered this unexpected change to the natural order of things. Having treated the shampooed and pomaded occupants of a *Boutique de Chiens* to his right with the contempt he clearly thought they deserved, he turned his attention to the vista on his left. As he did so the Parc Monceau loomed into view.

Resting his chin on his master's shoulder, Pommes Frites gazed soulfully through the offside window. Anyone watching could have been forgiven for assuming the worst. A hard done-by hound if ever there was one, possibly on its way to the knacker's yard.

Monsieur Pamplemousse glanced at his watch. It showed a minute or so before nine o'clock. It was his first day back at work after a successful tour of duty in Arcachon. No one would expect him to arrive at the office dead on time, least of all the Director, who had good cause to be in his debt in more ways than one. Had not Monsieur Leclercq specifically said that the choice of a next assignment lay with Monsieur Pamplemousse himself? The world – at least that part of it which lay within the boundaries of metropolitan France – was virtually his oyster.

In the meantime the sighing in his ear was becoming almost intolerable. To stop or not to stop? The question resolved itself almost immediately when an empty parking space suddenly materialised ahead of them.

Entering the Parc Monceau through a pair of vast and gilded ornamental wrought-iron gates, Monsieur Pamplemousse returned the salute of an elderly gendarme who appeared from behind a large rotunda. It was nice to know there were still those in the force who recognised him from his days with the Sûreté. All the same, he was glad he had thought to put Pommes Frites on a leash; the man already had his whistle at the ready.

Monsieur Pamplemousse tightened his grip on the lead as he joined a stream of commuters heading across the park towards the Champs Elysées. There was a large sand pit in the middle of the path leading off to his right and he sensed that Pommes Frites might have designs on it; designs which would undoubtedly have been legislated against on one of the many notice boards. It looked like a 'no go' area in all senses of the word. That being so, he led the way along a path to their left. Out of the corner of his eye he could see the gendarme still keeping a watchful eye on them. It was a case of better safe than sorry.

In the days to come Monsieur Pamplemousse would more than once fall to wondering what might have happened had he risked the gendarme's opprobrium and gone to his right. Would everything have been different?

As it was, he strolled on his way past large areas of begonias and between beds filled with marigolds and busy lizzies, blissfully unaware that he was setting in motion his involvement in a train of events as bizarre as any he had yet experienced.

It was a tranquil scene. Roses were in full bloom everywhere. Pigeons waddled to and fro as they foraged for unconsidered trifles; sparrows followed in their wake. Only the soft swish of water from hosepipes playing over the freshly mown grass and the occasional heavy breathing of passing joggers disturbed the peace.

Their route took them towards the *naumachia basin*, an artificial lake modelled, so it was said, after pools the ancient Romans were wont to construct in order to simulate mock naval battles. Ducks swam lazily back and forth, pausing every now and then in order to dip their beaks into the water. In the coming months the colonnades beyond the lake would form the background to many a fashionable wedding photograph, but for the moment it wasn't hard to picture it peopled by toga-clad citizens of the Roman Empire, idly helping themselves from bunches of grapes as they spurred their model boats on to victory over a late breakfast.

Had Monsieur Pamplemousse taken the path to the right that morning his thoughts might well have been on madeleines rather than ancient Rome, for had he not once read that Marcel Proust used to play in the sand with his friend Antoinette Fauve? Marcel Proust, whose most memorable work was inspired by the simple act of dipping a spoonful of madeleine cake crumbs into a cup of lime tea.

And if his thoughts had been on madeleines, then it was more than likely he would have spurned the Director's offer of a trip to the Camargue, opting instead for a chance to sample the culinary delights in and around Illiers-Combray, home territory of the illustrious writer.

Pommes Frites had no such romantic notions. As far as he was concerned water was for swimming in, ducks were meant to be eaten, and birds and joggers were there to be chased. Unable to do any of these things, he strained at his leash, anxious to explore pastures new.

Monsieur Pamplemousse knew how he felt. It was ridiculous really. It was only a matter of days since their return from Arcachon and already he, too, was feeling restless. It was hard to put a finger on the cause. Perhaps it had to with the feeling of holidays in the air. All the way along from the Place de Clichy waiters had been busy putting out extra tables and chairs ready for *déjeuner*, anxious to make the most of things before the annual migration out of Paris began. Men in green overalls had been busy with their brooms. Pavements glistened from being freshly machine-washed. It was rather as though everything was being spruced up and made ready for putting into store. In a few weeks time Paris, at least as far as its residents were concerned, would be empty.

Studiously averting his gaze from the shadowy figures practising Tai Chi behind some bushes, he moved on round the gardens and stood for a while contemplating the spot where, on the 22 October 1797, a certain Monsieur Jacques Garnerin, the world's first parachutist, had caused consternation amongst the local populace by literally falling out of the sky. It didn't help.

Monsieur P... feeling of unrest lasted all
the w... round the Arc de Triomphe
... hat it needed but a turn of
t... in any direction he chose;
n... s that sort of morning.

... und for the second time,
he ... headed towards the pont
de ... car park beneath the
Espl...

A f... ff the rue Fabert and
applie... late let into the wall.
In resp... pushed open a small
door ma... into a courtyard on
the far si... tain, lay *Le Guide's*
headquar...

Even ol... th, OR & Procedure Check-in Area ...ug, the gatekeeper, seemed to have
caught the ...ug. The window of his little room just inside
the entrance was wide open: an unprecedented event. No
doubt if he caught a cold they would all suffer the
consequences.

Crossing the courtyard, Monsieur Pamplemousse
entered the main building through the large plate-glass
revolving doors. He exchanged greetings with the recep-
tionist and then, ignoring the lift, bounded up the main
stairs two at a time.

The Inspectors' office on the third floor was empty. It
was the time of year when most of his colleagues were
scattered far and wide across the length and breadth of
France, searching out new restaurants, checking on long-
established ones, double-checking those earmarked for
promotion, or in some cases demotion, following up
unsolicited letters of praise or complaint.

Panting a little after his exertions, Monsieur Pamplemousse settled down at his desk and started to go through
the contents of his In-Tray. There was the usual assort-
ment of odds and ends. Some queries from Madame
Grante about past expenses – he put those on one side to

deal with later – she had yet to see the extras he had accumulated in Arcachon; they would need *Monsieur le Directeur*'s approval before he even dared broach the subject. Explaining how and why Pommes Frites had come to bury one of *Le Guide*'s issue camera lenses in the sand at Cap Ferret would not be easy: worse than filling in an accident report. Lips would be compressed. Unanswerable questions would be posed. Pleading that the lens had been in a pocket of his best suit which had also been engulfed by the incoming tide would be a waste of time.

There was a note from Trigaux in the Art Department saying a film he'd wanted processed was ready for collection. Bernard had left him a wine list containing several sale items marked with a cross. Bernard had connections in the wine trade and an eye for a bargain. Truffert had returned a tape he'd borrowed – *Gerry Mulligan Meets Ben Webster*.

Reaching across, Monsieur Pamplemousse felt in his tray in case he had missed anything. His fingers made contact with a small plastic envelope. A tag bearing his name was attached to the outside. Printed in red across the top were the words SECRET ET CONFIDENTIEL. Tearing open the top of the packet, he upended it over his blotting pad. Bottle was too grand a word for the object which fell out. True it was made of brown glass, but it was so small there was no room for a label, nor was there anything inside the envelope to say who had put it there in the first place or why.

He held the object up to the light, but it was impossible to see if there was any liquid inside. He decided it must contain something because it had a tiny glass stopper kept in place by a band of shrink plastic.

Taking a corkscrew from his pocket, Monsieur Pamplemousse released the knife blade and made a nick in the band. Still half-suspecting one of his colleagues might be playing a prank, he gingerly removed the stopper and applied it to the end of his nose. It was a perfume of some kind. Mildly assertive, yet with an underlying promise of other things to come; it was hard to put a word to it. Sensual? Decadent? That was it – decadent.

Analysing it as one might a glass of wine, isolating one part from another, he first of all registered musk. Beyond that he thought he could detect the smell of incense. There were spices too, spices . . . roses? . . . perhaps a damask rose? Certainly flowers of some kind. Jasmine? There was more than a hint of oakmoss. He added coriander to his list before he gave up. Doubtless there were many, many more, but it would need an expert and highly trained nose to isolate them. The overall effect wasn't unpleasant: very much the reverse. But why he should be the recipient of such a strange gift he hadn't the remotest idea. Perhaps someone was trying to tell him something?

He picked up the phial and dribbled the contents over the back of his other hand in the way that he'd seen women do when they were testing samples in a shop. Rather more came out than he had intended. It trickled off on to the desk and he was about to reach for his handkerchief when he thought better of it. Doucette might suspect the worst.

Catching sight of Pommes Frites stirring in his sleep, Monsieur Pamplemousse hastily crossed to the nearest window and flung it open. He had no wish for anyone to come in and catch him smelling to high heaven.

He was in the act of waving his arm to and fro when he happened to catch sight of a familiar car drawing into its official parking place to the right of the main entrance. The solitary occupant alighted and was about to slam the door shut when he glanced up as though to check the weather.

Monsieur Pamplemousse froze. It was too late to withdraw his arm, so he did the next best thing – he converted the waving motion into a form of salutation. The greeting was not returned. Instead, the driver stared

7

up at him for several seconds, then reopened the door of his car and reached for a telephone on the centre console.

Closing the window, Monsieur Pamplemousse hurried back to his desk. He hardly had time to settle down again before the telephone rang. It was Véronique, the Director's secretary.

'Monsieur Pamplemousse. Monsieur Leclercq wishes to see you in his office.'

'Now?'

'*Oui. Tout de suite.*'

'Did he sound . . .?'

Véronique anticipated his question. '*Non. Au contraire.* He sounded very cheerful. He simply said as soon as possible. He is on his way up now. If you hurry you may beat him to it.'

Monsieur Pamplemousse hastily replaced the stopper in the phial and parcelled it up inside an envelope. Then he opened a drawer. The mystery would have to wait.

He glanced down. Pommes Frites' nose was twitching and there was the suspicion of a smile playing on his lips. It seemed a pity to disturb him.

Véronique made a thumbs-down gesture as Monsieur Pamplemousse entered the Director's outer office. Behind an open door he could see her boss already seated at his desk. Clearly the race had gone to the one with the private lift.

'*Entrez*, Aristide. *Entrez.*' Catching sight of his subordinate, Monsieur Leclercq rose to his feet and after a brief but undeniably warm handshake motioned towards an armchair.

Monsieur Pamplemousse did as he was bidden. Véronique was right. The signs were not bad. In fact, his chief looked in an unusually sunny mood.

'I trust you are fully recovered from your stay in Arcachon, Aristide?' he began.

'I think I have seen enough sand to last me for a while, *Monsieur*. The dunes are unbelievably large.'

The Director sniffed. 'I take it you have been at the bottle already.'

Monsieur Pamplemousse looked suitably injured. 'I assure you, *Monsieur*, that not a drop has passed my lips since yesterday evening.'

'No, no, Pamplemousse, you misunderstand me. I was referring to the sample fragrance I asked Véronique to place in your tray. Tell me what you think of it. I value your opinion.'

'It is . . . unusual . . .' Monsieur Pamplemousse hesitated. Something in the tone of the Director's voice prompted him to leave his options open for the time being.

'It is not one I have come across before,' he added cautiously.

The Director closed the door to his outer office and then glanced quickly round the room to make doubly certain the rest were properly shut. 'That, Aristide, is because it is not yet on the market. The launch date has yet to be fixed. Field trials are still in progress.

'A "come-hither" perfume would you say? Hard to resist?'

'I have not put it to the test, *Monsieur*.'

'Madame Grante has not been chasing you down the corridors overcome by barely concealed passion?'

'No, *Monsieur*. I am glad to say she has not. I came as soon as I received Véronique's call.'

The Director looked mildly disappointed. He gave another sniff and retreated towards the window.

While his chief's back was turned Monsieur Pamplemousse automatically glanced at the desk to see if it offered any clues as to why he had been summoned. Somewhat to his surprise he saw there was a translation of the works of the great Roman cookery writer, Apicius, lying open. Alongside it was a paperback book. As far as he could make out from the title on the spine it was a glossary of film terms.

Rather more ominously, he also caught sight of a P.27 – the standard form used by *Le Guide* in order to record personal details relating to members of staff. He was too far away to see whether or not his own name was at the top. The answer was not long in coming.

Having made himself comfortable, the Director picked up the form.

'I have been going through your records, Aristide. I see you spent some time attached to the fraud squad while you were with the *Sûreté*.'

Monsieur Pamplemousse gave a non-committal '*oui*'. He wondered what was coming next.

'No doubt you learned a great deal about perfume while you were there?'

'It was not really my area, *Monsieur*. I was mostly concerned with food. Food and drink. Unscrupulous fishmongers who resort to varnishing the eyes of their wares when they grow stale. As for drink, believe me, *Monsieur*, you will find more ways of spelling Byrrh and Pernod in the Musée de Contrefaçon than you would have thought possible. People read what they expect to read. But I know there is a section devoted to perfume; there are numerous examples of passing off – names like Chanel become Cherel, or even Chinarl. Dior-Dior turned up once as Dora-Dora. Nina Ricci, Guy Laroche, Givenchy, even Guérlain have all suffered in their time.

'With a world-wide market for perfume worth tens of billions of francs, counterfeiting is big business these days. Perfume is the reflection of many people's dreams. It offers the promise of excitement in their lives: a touch of wickedness. And where there are desires to be satisfied corruption is never far away.'

The Director nodded.

'Tell me, Aristide, talking of wickedness, what do you know about sin?'

Monsieur Pamplemousse suddenly caught on. Although his annual increment wasn't due until October,

10

the Director must be ahead of himself; clearing the decks before his summer holiday. At such times he had a penchant for plying members of staff with trick questions. Two could play at that game. He, Pamplemousse, was more than ready. It was simply a case of avoiding the obvious at all costs.

'Sin was a fortress in ancient Egypt, *Monsieur*; situated in the Nile Delta. It is famous because in the reign of Hezekiah, a certain general by the name of Sennacherib led an attack on it which had to be abandoned because a plague of field mice ate up his archers' bowstrings.'

Monsieur Pamplemousse felt pleased with himself. It was strange how these things stuck in one's mind. It was something he had learned at school in a year when the Auvergne had suffered a similar plague. His teacher had used it as an illustration of how even very tiny creatures can sometimes change the course of history.

He felt tempted to say 'ask me another', but something in the way the Director's lips were pursed caused him to think better of it. There were times when his chief's moods and intentions were hard to judge and he seemed less than happy with the reply.

'And Les Baux-de-Provence, Pamplemousse. What can you tell me about Les Baux?'

Monsieur Pamplemousse thought for a moment. He doubted if the Director expected him to eulogise on L'Oustau de Baumanière, Monsieur Raymond Thuilier's world-famous restaurant on the lower slopes; a restaurant where, in 1972, the Queen of England had dined on sea bass *en croûte*, followed by lamb, and strawberries and cream. The menu had stayed in his mind because shortly afterwards Doucette had cooked it for him as a surprise.

'Les Baux, *Monsieur*? Les Baux is a strange geological excrescence in the Apilles north of the Camargue; a natural fortress. The warlords of Les Baux are legendary. They claimed to be descended from Balthazar. It was there that another unfortunate incident took place,

11

although this time it hadn't to do with mice. The story goes that the Duke of Guise was staying for the night, and having indulged himself with too much wine at dinner he ordered a salute to be fired every time he proposed a toast. Unfortunately the very first time he raised his glass the canon nearest to him exploded. Although there is a tombstone bearing his name in a cemetery at Arles, it is merely a token gesture. In reality the Duke himself was scattered over a wide area.

'Another interesting fact is that the mineral bauxite was discovered nearby and was named after the village. As I am sure *Monsieur* knows, bauxite is a basic material of the aluminium industry . . .'

Suddenly aware of a drumming noise coming from the desk in front of him, Monsieur Pamplemousse broke off.

The Director heaved a deep sigh. 'Pamplemousse, I yield to no one in my admiration of the depth of your knowledge on a variety of subjects. However, I was not asking for a history lesson.'

But Monsieur Pamplemousse was not to be stopped that easily. 'I am sorry, *Monsieur*. I was lucky with my teacher. Although it was only a village school, she had a flair for bringing things to life.' Even as he spoke he wondered if deep down he wasn't trying to score over his chief, whose education had followed a very different path; a path available only to the rich and privileged.

He closed his eyes for a moment, the better to draw on his store of knowledge. 'Another of her favourite stories concerned Leonardo da Vinci. Possibly it was apocryphal – there are so many – but it tells of how he invented a giant watercress cutter which ran amuck outside the Sforza palace the very first time he tried it out and killed six members of the kitchen staff and three gardeners.'

Monsieur Pamplemousse paused. The Director looked as though he would have dearly liked to get his hands on such a machine himself.

'Tell me, Pamplemousse, to return to my first question,

12

did she at the same time instil in you a knowledge of the seven deadly sins? Can you by any chance still enumerate them?'

But if the Director was hoping to win a round he was unlucky. This time Monsieur Pamplemousse didn't even bother closing his eyes.

'Pride, *Monsieur*. Wrath, envy, lust, gluttony, avarice and sloth.'

In spite of everything a look of grudging admiration crossed the Director's face. 'You were indeed lucky with your teacher, Aristide,' he said gruffly. 'Most people can hardly name more than two or three.'

'It was not my teacher who taught me about the seven deadly sins, *Monsieur*. It was the *curé*. He lectured the congregation on the subject most Sundays. He was of the opinion that all seven were rife in the village.'

'Aaah!' The Director sat in silence for a moment or two.

'I expect, Aristide,' he said at last, 'you are wondering where my enquiries are leading?'

Monsieur Pamplemousse thought the matter over carefully before replying. The Director's questions had been so diverse it was hard to find a common denominator. In desperation he glanced at the desk again and took in the open copy of Apicius's culinary work.

'Monsieur is gathering material for a spoof guide?'

The Director glared at Monsieur Pamplemousse for a moment, then he reached over and slammed the book shut.

'No, Pamplemousse,' he said crossly. 'I am not.' Rising to his feet with the air of a man badly in need of a drink he headed towards a cupboard on the far side of the room.

As he opened the door a light came on revealing a wine bucket, its sides glistening with beads of ice-cold sweat. The gold foil-covered neck of a bottle protruded from the top. Monsieur Pamplemousse recognised his favourite marque of champagne – Gosset. Clearly his being summoned to the top floor was not, as he had at first supposed, a spur of the moment decision.

'I have been trying to think of a way of expressing my thanks for all you did in Arcachon, Pamplemousse.'

Monsieur Pamplemousse made a suitably deprecating noise.

'It was far from being nothing,' insisted the Director. 'You averted a disaster of the first magnitude. Elsie is a lovely girl, but to have had her on our staff would have been disruptive to say the least, not to mention the problems I might have encountered *chez* Leclercq.'

Monsieur Pamplemousse was of the opinion that the Director's one-time *au pair* had never entertained the slightest intention of becoming an Inspector, but he remained silent.

'I have been considering your next assignment, Aristide. I had been toying with the idea of sending you to the Rhône Valley; Bocuse, Pic, and so on, but I have since been wondering how you would feel about going further south.' The Director handed him a glass. 'Loudier was really due to go, but in the circumstances I think you are the better man.'

'The circumstances, *Monsieur*?' Once again it all sounded a little too casual for comfort.

'Circumstances are like carpenters, Aristide. They alter cases. You may, of course, go anywhere you choose.'

'Anywhere, *Monsieur*?'

'A promise is a promise. It is the least I can do. However, before you decide, I have something else in mind, something a little out of the ordinary which I am sure will be right up your *rue*.'

While the Director was returning to his seat, Monsieur Pamplemousse sipped the champagne thoughtfully. It was a Brut Réserve. A wine of quality, with over 400 years of family tradition behind it. He wondered what was coming next.

The Director fortified himself with a generous gulp

14

from his own glass before he resumed.

'Earlier in the week I was dining with some friends and quite by chance found myself sitting next to the wife of one of our major *couturiers*. One thing led to another – I passed some comment on the perfume she was wearing – and she, for her part, was not unimpressed by my dissertation on the dish we had been served – saddle of lamb with truffles, chestnuts and a delicious *purée* of mushroom tart.

'For the time being the name of her husband's company must remain a closely guarded secret, but I can tell you they are about to launch a new perfume. It is to be called, quite simply, Excess – spelt XS.

'Soon, those two letters will be appearing on hoardings all over France. They will act as a teaser before the campaign proper.

'A major part of the launch involves the making of a series of commercials based on stories from the Bible. Work has already begun. Several episodes are already in the can. They will become classics of their kind. There is a star-studded cast and a budget of over 100 million francs. If I tell you they have engaged the services of no less a person than Von Strudel as the director you will appreciate the magnitude of the project.'

'Von Strudel, *Monsieur*? I must admit I didn't realise he was still alive.'

'There are unkind people in the business,' said the Director, 'who would say that even Von Strudel himself wasn't entirely convinced of the fact when they first approached him. He has been living the life of a recluse in his native Austria ever since biblical films priced themselves out of the market. He is, nevertheless, one of the greatest authorities on the *genre*.

'If he has a fault it is that he has become a little out of touch with present-day costs. He is not blessed, as we are, with a Madame Grante looking over his shoulder and he is already considerably over budget. Over budget and for one reason and another behind schedule.

'But to return to the dinner. The long and the short of it is that at the end of the evening my companion made me a proposal I could hardly refuse.'

'It happens, *Monsieur*.' Monsieur Pamplemousse assumed his man of the world tones as he drained his glass.

The Director clucked impatiently. 'It was not that sort of proposal, Pamplemousse,' he growled as he took the hint and reached for the bottle. 'Although I must say your reply does lead me to feel that in dispatching you to Les Baux I have made the right choice.'

'Les Baux, *Monsieur*?'

The Director sighed. 'Aristide, I do wish you would break yourself of the habit of repeating everything I say. It can be very irritating.

'The reason I am suggesting you go to Les Baux is because they are badly in need of an adviser. As I am sure you know, Pamplemousse, Von Strudel was renowned for his scenes of lust and gluttony. Naturally when I heard those two key words your name sprang immediately to mind. I can think of no one better qualified to advise on both those subjects.'

'*Merci, Monsieur*,' said Monsieur Pamplemousse drily. 'And what precisely am I expected to advise on?'

'Anything to do with food, Pamplemousse,' said the Director grandly. 'Anything and everything. Food as it was in Roman times. Food in the Bible. The essential culinary ingredients for an orgy if the need arises.

'I need hardly tell you that to be associated with such a project, even in a minor way, to have our name mentioned when awards are given out at the Cannes Festival, will be a considerable *plume* in our *chapeau*.'

Despite his misgivings, Monsieur Pamplemousse felt his mind getting into gear. It was an exciting prospect and no mistake.

'I believe the Romans were very keen on edible dormice, *Monsieur*. They first of all fattened them on nuts in special earthenware jars and then they stuffed them with minced pork and pine kernels.'

The Director looked dubious.

'Pamplemousse, I hardly think dormice, however edible they might be, would go down well with the cast. However, there are other things.' He picked up the copy of Apicius and turned to a marked page. '*Par exemple*, I see they ate bread and honey for *petit déjeuner*. Milk was strictly for invalids. Instead, they used to dip the bread in a glass of wine.'

He snapped the book shut. 'You may borrow this if it is of any help. Von Strudel has a reputation for being a stickler for detail. That is why I wish you to go, Pamplemousse. We must not let the side down.'

'With respect, *Monsieur*, if Von Strudel is such a stickler for detail and he is dealing with biblical times, why does he not shoot the film in the Middle East where most of the events took place?'

The Director dismissed the suggestion with a wave of his hand.

'The cost of the insurance would be too great. That part of the world is in a constant state of turmoil. Also, there is another reason. Von Strudel is not exactly welcome on the shores of Israel. His name has unhappy associations with certain events which took place in Europe during the last war. There are those who, some fifty years after the event, are still out to exact revenge. Even at the age of eighty-five life is sweet.

'Besides, we are not talking about real life. We are talking about make-believe. There are details and there are mere details. The simple fact, as I understand it, is that the Art Director happened to be staying with a friend at L'Oustau de Baumanière and he fell in love with the setting. In his mind's eye it has already been transformed into the Mount of Olives.'

The Director gazed dreamily into space. 'Mangetout is

17

playing the part of the Virgin Mary. Before I met Chantal, Aristide, I was very much in love with her. She was France's answer to Rita Hayworth, with the added advantage of being half her age. I still have a signed photograph I sent away for. I remember the feeling of disappointment that came over me when I found the signature had been printed. It destroyed something very special and private.'

'There was always hope, *Monsieur*.'

'The magic of the silver screen, Aristide. We all thought we were the only one.' The Director hesitated. 'That still doesn't answer my question.'

Monsieur Pamplemousse felt himself weakening. As an avid cinemagoer, the chance of being involved in the making of a film – even a commercial – was too good to turn down. If he didn't want to talk himself out of a job any protests he made from now on would need to be of a token variety.

'Madame Pamplemousse will not be pleased. As you know, *Monsieur*, I have only just returned from Arcachon.'

'Madame Pamplemousse is welcome to accompany you,' said the Director generously. 'I am sure she can be budgeted for. We will think up a title. She can be your AAO. Assistant to the Adviser on Orgies.'

'That is kind of you, *Monsieur*,' said Monsieur Pamplemousse hastily, 'but that won't be necessary. In any case Doucette would not be happy staying at L'Oustau. It is a little too *chic* for her tastes. She would be worrying all the time about what to wear in the evenings.'

The Director dismissed his protest. 'The problem will not arise, Pamplemousse. The hotel has been taken over lock, stock and barrel by the film company. They are using it as their production headquarters.'

'How about its off-shoot further down the hill, *Monsieur* – La Cabro d'Or?'

'That is being occupied by lesser mortals: those who I

18

believe are known somewhat prosaically in the film business as gaffers and grips.'

Monsieur Pamplemousse puckered his brow in thought. 'There are not many other hotels in the area.'

'*Pas de problème*, Pamplemousse. You have been allotted a caravan.'

'A caravan?' Monsieur Pamplemousse tried hard to keep the note of disappointment from his voice. 'In that case Madame Pamplemousse will certainly not be accompanying me. We have an agreement.'

Memories of a caravan holiday they had spent in the Dordogne soon after they were married came flooding back. It had been impossible to boil a kettle without first taking something else apart. Going to bed at night and getting up again in the morning had been a nightmare. They had both sworn never again. And that was long before Pommes Frites appeared on the scene.

'There are caravans, Pamplemousse,' said the Director, 'and there are caravans. Wait until you see what yours will be like.' Opening a desk drawer, he removed a large, glossy brochure.

'A whole fleet of these was ordered from America. They have been strategically placed so as to form the nerve centre of the whole operation. Make-up, wardrobe, rest rooms . . . you will be surrounded by other experts in their various fields. There is even a resident chef.'

Monsieur Pamplemousse suppressed a whistle as he gazed at the picture on the cover. It was an artist's impression and therefore one had to accept that certain aspects of the scene were probably grossly over-exaggerated; the man standing on the steps of the caravan clasping a glass in his hand must have been at least seven feet tall – he would have needed to duck in order to get through the doorway – if, indeed, he was capable of bending at all; the surrounding foliage was a shade too luxuriant even by Californian standards.

However, it was the final artistic embellishment which

caused Monsieur Pamplemousse to make up his mind without any further hesitation. There was a bloodhound sitting on the grass outside the caravan and it bore an uncanny resemblance to Pommes Frites. The likeness was so great, for a moment he almost suspected the Director of having engineered the whole thing. He dismissed the thought from his mind. There would not have been time. Clearly, the whole thing was meant.

'So what is it to be, Aristide? *Oui ou non*?'

'I think you may safely assume, *Monsieur*, that the answer is *oui*.'

'Good man! I knew I could rely on you.' The Director poured out the remains of the champagne and having gulped down the contents of his own glass with a haste bordering on the indecent, he reached inside the drawer again and withdrew a long white envelope. 'In fact, I was so convinced you wouldn't let me down I had Véronique prepare an introductory letter to Von Strudel himself.'

'*Merci, Monsieur*.' Taking the hint, Monsieur Pamplemousse pocketed the letter, downed his own champagne, and made for the door. As he turned the knob he felt the Director's hand on his shoulder.

'Take care, Aristide. In the meantime I would strongly advise you to stay away from the typing pool. One of the major selling points of the new perfume is that a little XS goes a long way and I suspect you may have been over-generous. Portion control on your part is sadly lacking.

'And if I may offer one final word of advice. When you get to Les Baux watch out for the "best boys". I have no idea what their precise function is, or why they should receive a credit for doing it, but whenever their names appear on the screen I always fear the worst.'

Monsieur Pamplemousse was aware of a certain excitement in his step as he left the Director's office. He couldn't wait to show the brochure to Pommes Frites.

Waving goodbye to Véronique, he caught a whiff of XS

and wondered for a moment whether he should put the Director's theory to the test and try it out on Madame Grante, perhaps even take a short cut to her office via the typing pool, waving to the girls as he went?

Reason prevailed. He slowed down as he made his way along the corridor. His inner warning system was already hard at work. Thinking back on the meeting it seemed too good to be true. In retrospect, the conversation – the champagne on ice – the little tidbits of information dropped in here and there – had all felt too pat, too carefully rehearsed.

By the time Monsieur Pamplemousse reached the lift he had a growing presentiment that watching out for 'best boys' might well turn out to be the least of his problems in the days to come.

2
DINNER WITH A BANG

Monsieur Pamplemousse's caravan manifested itself in
the shape of an American custom-built Star Wagon trailer
of vast proportions, some twelve metres in length by
perhaps two and a half metres wide. It was one of a
number parked beneath a row of plane trees on the lower
slopes of Les Baux-de-Provence. They were all of a luxury
beyond anything he could have imagined.

Having turned off the A7 Autoroute du Soleil at
Cavaillon, hot and tired after the long drive from Paris, he
had approached his destination via St Rémy and the D5.
His first sighting of the film company's location came as
he rounded a bend in the twisting road which skirted the
old town of Les Baux. The detritus of previous days'
filming awaited collection – a discarded city of partly
dismantled sets, façades of buildings, transport of all
kinds – bullock carts, carriages of various shapes and
sizes, a chariot or two, plus a motley collection of vans,
lorries and cars. Beyond that lay sundry pieces of film
equipment – camera cranes, lighting gantries, switch-
boards, generators spewing out thick cables in all directions. In the distance, although there was no water to be
seen, was what looked like the carcass of a large boat left
high and dry by a tide which had long since receded never
to return.

Monsieur Pamplemousse braked sharply and a crowd

of spectators sprawled across barriers set up at the side of the road turned their heads as his car ground to a halt.

A buzz of excitement went up as someone registered an official sticker on his windscreen. Faces peered in through the open windows as others parted to let him through. Autograph books appeared as if by magic. Fingers pointed towards the passenger seat. Never one to miss a trick, Pommes Frites assumed a faintly regal air while his master conferred with a uniformed man at the entrance to the site. Cameras clicked as a barrier was raised and they were waved on their way.

Monsieur Pamplemousse drove a short distance along a track indicated by the guard. He parked his 2CV in the shade of an olive tree and then set about unloading their belongings from the back seat. Cameras went into action again as Pommes Frites climbed out after him, stretched, and then obeyed an urgent call of nature. Photographically speaking, it was clearly a case of grasping at straws. In the fullness of time albums the world over would testify to the fact that until their arrival action had been thin on the ground. Entering into the spirit of things, Pommes Frites turned his best side towards the cameras.

Entering the trailer by what turned out to be the back door, Monsieur Pamplemousse found himself in a make-up area. Behind the make-up table itself there was a large mirror lit by rows of small, unshaded light bulbs along the sides and top. The reflection showed he had already caught the sun.

Laid out on a towel in front of the mirror were the tools of the trade; a selection of brushes in sanitised wrappings, tissues, sponges, eyebrow pencils, mascara, a jar of cleansing cream. On the other side of the room there was a telephone, and a colour television.

A curtained-off area to one side of a large wardrobe revealed a marine-style toilet and a full-size bath. The temptation to take a cold shower was hard to resist; the last 100 kilometres or so of the journey down had been like driving through a furnace. Air-conditioning was not one of the *Deux Chevaux*'s optional extras – unless you counted having the roof rolled back.

Curiosity got the better of Monsieur Pamplemousse. Opening a full-length mirrored door beyond the bath, he found himself in a kitchen area complete with a Westinghouse refrigerator, a Sharp Carousel II convection microwave oven and a gas cooking hob. Alongside the hob was a stainless steel double sink unit. On a tiny shelf to the left of the oven stood a copy of Barbara Kafka's *Microwave Gourmet Healthstyle Cookbook* – an all-embracing title if ever he'd seen one, but a welcome sight nevertheless. The word microwave was banned *chez* Pamplemousse and the whole process remained a mystery to him.

There was a cupboard with a range of pots and pans and a shelf of dry foodstuffs. To his left was an alcove with a small face-to-face dinette. In the centre of the built-in table stood a glazed pottery bowl containing sprigs of broom; a gathering of golden butterflies.

Monsieur Pamplemousse opened the refrigerator door. Someone had done their job well. It was replete with fruit and vegetables; soft drinks – fruit juices and mineral water – tins of beer and a supply of local wine – Terres Blanches and some Listel *gris-de-gris*.

There was red wine in a rack above the working surface – some Châteauneuf-du-Pape and a bottle or two of Cabernet-Sauvignon: Mont Caume from the Bandol. Alongside it was a rack of culinary implements. They looked unused.

On an upper shelf stood an unopened tin of black olives from a Monsieur André Arnaud of nearby Fontvieille.

Having filled a bowl with some ice-cold water from a tap attached to the refrigerator, Monsieur Pamplemousse helped himself to an equally cold Budweiser while Pommes Frites noisily slaked his thirst.

Another door led to the main living-room. The beige carpet, striped with bars of sunlight filtering through a venetian blind covering a picture window at the far end, felt thick underfoot. An elevated area beneath the window supported a double bed.

Closer inspection revealed a second colour television receiver, a larger one this time – a Mitsubishi with a matching B82 video recorder – a Sony stereo cassette player, yet another telephone and a FAX machine. He could hardly complain of being cut off from the world.

After the canvas front seat of his *Deux Chevaux* the bed felt deeply luxurious. From somewhere overhead came a welcome draught of cool air. It accounted for the faint hum of a generator which he'd heard on entering the trailer. Come night-time it would probably be the usual toss-up between being kept awake by the noise, or open windows and the risk being bitten. Nearby Arles was reckoned to be the mosquito capital of France. No doubt they had plenty of relatives in the surrounding country-side. The news of fresh arrivals from the north would travel fast.

Monsieur Pamplemousse lay where he was for a moment or two, then he reached across and parted the blind. Dotted here and there were signs of civilisation – the odd patch of terracotta roof tiles or an occasional scattering of sheep or goats left behind for whatever reason while the rest of the flock enjoyed a summer diet of wild herbs in the surrounding uplands – but mostly the limestone terrain was bare and forbidding. Val d'Enfer – Hell Valley – wild and unruly; in the old days it must have earned its name. The light was dazzlingly clear. No wonder Van Gogh had been drawn to the area. A thermometer leading from an outside sensor was nudging 32°C. The thermometer inside the trailer showed a pleasant 19°C.

Pommes Frites came into the room, padded silently round on a tour of inspection, sniffed and went out again.

Monsieur Pamplemousse took the hint. He got up and began unpacking his bags, most of which were filled with reference books he had literally thrown in at the last moment; the Director's copy of Apicius, and as many other books relating to the subject as he had been able to lay his hands on at short notice. They took their place among a scattering of others on a mahogany shelf at the end of the bed.

Leaving the rest of the unpacking for the time being, he fed the cassette player with the tape Truffert had returned to him. As the sound of Billy Strayhorn's 'Chelsea Bridge' filled the air he squeezed a tube of *Eau Sauvage* gel into the bath and turned on the taps.

Anxious to share the news of his good fortune, he lay back in the foam for a while, composing a fax to the Director, then rapidly amended it. There was no point in making life sound too attractive. If Madame Grante got wind of it she would go through his expenses with a fine tooth comb. Something along the lines of 'TEDIOUS JOURNEY DOWN, BUT ARRIVED SAFELY. DESPITE INTENSE HEAT, WORK GOING ACCORDING TO PLAN' would suffice. If he dispatched it as late as possible before going to bed that night the automatic recording of time of origin might earn him Brownie points.

That problem out of the way, he had to admit to a feeling of unease. Even the music, far from giving him the lift it normally did, had a reverse effect. The sheer professionalism of the way Mulligan and Webster played together sowed seeds of doubt in his mind about his own capabilities for the task ahead. Despite his performance in the Director's office, all he really knew about the period he was supposed to advise on could have been written on the back of a spoon. He had to admit with a sense of shame that he didn't even know the date of the crucifixion. As for what had been eaten at the last supper . . . the few books he had glanced through conveniently glossed over the subject.

It was another hour and a quarter before Monsieur Pamplemousse finished his ablutions. Allowing the last soulful strains of Ben Webster's rendering of 'Blues in B Flat' to die away, he looked at his watch. It showed nearly seven o'clock. There was a click as the machine switched itself off.

Emerging from the trailer he had an immediate reminder of just how hot the Camargue could be in July, even at that time of the day. It was as though he had opened an oven door. At least the Mistral wasn't blowing.

An immediate reminder of Pommes Frites' whereabouts came via a loud bang from inside the trailer.

Monsieur Pamplemousse turned to go back up the steps, and as he did so he had a pleasant surprise. If only Doucette could have been there to see it too – she would have been very proud. He reached up to touch the name board screwed to the top of the door. The 'M' on M. PAMPLEMOUSSE still felt slightly tacky. Flecks of dust had stuck to the white paint. A salutary warning, Hollywood style, that nothing is for ever, least of all in the world of make-believe. A few strokes of a brush and he would cease to exist. He wondered how many other names had graced that very same board, and whose for that matter?

'Hullo there! *Comment ça va*?'

Looking round, Monsieur Pamplemousse spotted a lone figure sitting at a table beneath a large sunshade advertising Ricard. There was a matching bottle on the table, together with a jug of water and some glasses.

'*Bien, merci.*' Returning the wave, he followed Pommes Frites along a path worn by the occupants of the neighbouring trailers. On his way he stole a glance at the names on some of the doors. Mostly they meant nothing to him. Brother Angelo – he guessed he must be an adviser of some kind; Gilbert Beaseley – the name rang the faintest of bells; he spotted Mangetout's quarters a little way back from the others. Alongside it were two other unmarked trailers. All three had their blinds drawn.

The person who had called out the greeting rose to his feet as Monsieur Pamplemousse drew near. He was wearing a white shirt, the long sleeves of which were folded back rather than rolled, a cravat, immaculately pressed beige trousers and suede boots. If Monsieur Pamplemousse hadn't already guessed from the accent, his nationality radiated from every pore. He was clutching a half empty glass in long, thin fingers. From his demeanour it looked as though it wasn't the first that evening.

Monsieur Pamplemousse accepted the proffered hand. That, too, was droopy. 'Gilbert Beaseley . . .' The greying quiff of hair casually tossed to one side matched his eyes. 'You may have heard of me. Writer. Go anywhere. Do anything. Distance no object. Masonics and biblical films a speciality.'

'I have seen your name.'

'I saw yours being put up, too. Welcome to Babylon.' Monsieur Pamplemousse's suit was noted with approval. 'I see you haven't gone native yet. Good chap. Must keep up the standards.'

'I came away in a hurry,' said Monsieur Pamplemousse simply. It was all too true. Thoughtlessly, he hadn't even bothered to pack any short-sleeved shirts. Doucette would raise her eyes to Heaven when she found out.

'Would you care to join me in an *apéritif*?'

Monsieur Pamplemousse hesitated. 'You look as though you are expecting company . . .'

'Not expecting . . . hoping. There is a crisis Ark-wise and I have been deserted.'

Refusal being clearly impossible, Monsieur Pamplemousse lowered himself into the remaining chair. As he did so he gave a start. Surprise gave way to embarrassment. The noise was loud, clear and unmistakable.

Gilbert Beaseley looked away, made a languid effort at swotting a passing fly and edged his own chair slightly away from the table.

Monsieur Pamplemousse shifted uneasily. The noise was repeated.

'*Pardon.*' The word came out automatically: an admission of guilt where none existed.

'Not at all.' Beaseley beamed at him. 'Are you taking anything for it?'

'It is nothing . . .' Monsieur Pamplemousse broke off. It was too late to deny responsibility even though his conscience was clear. The damage was done. He sat very still.

Pommes Frites eyed his master with interest for a moment or two. Then, before any attempt was made to shift the blame in his direction – as had been known on past occasions – he set off on a voyage of exploration. There were signs of activity down by the boat. Lights were coming on. A solitary dove winged its way low overhead, then turned and flew back again. It all looked worthy of investigation.

Gilbert Beaseley glanced after him. 'I see you've brought your own bodyguard. Very wise. I wish I had. Is he an only one? He hasn't a friend I could borrow?'

'It is not as simple as that,' said Monsieur Pamplemousse. 'He is unique. I do not know where I would be without him.'

'Pity. Everybody in this business ought to have a stand-in. You never know.'

Monsieur Pamplemousse forbore to ask why and the subject was abruptly changed as his host reached for the bottle.

'Forgive me. I'm being neglectful. I'm afraid you find Gilbert Beaseley not at his best. I should make the most of me. I may not last until morning.' He pushed a stiff measure of pastis across the table. 'I will leave you to do the necessary.'

'*Merci.*' Monsieur Pamplemousse removed a perforated spoon from one of the glasses, added a knob of white sugar, and began adding water from the jug slowly and carefully, drop by drop, partly for the sake of the ritual and partly because he feared a repeat performance of the dreaded noise. The water was satisfactorily cold and they both watched while the colourless liquid turned a tawny-yellow. Hoping to achieve a classic 5:1 ratio, *à la Marseillaise*, he was disappointed. It was as he feared; the helping of *pastis* had been more than generous.

'So you are a writer? I am sorry, I am afraid I have not read any of your works.'

Gilbert Beaseley sighed. 'My penetration of the French market is, I fear, fairly minimal. The sad fact is, many of my titles lose in the translation. They had great difficulty with my very first work – *Whatever Happened to the Sandcastles I Built when I was Young? It ended up as Châteaux* and everyone thought it was a book on doll's houses. It put them off buying any more. It was a slight work – a mere fifty pages in free verse – but I like to think it caught the mood of the Swinging Sixties in England – the end of it anyway, when people were eager to wallow in nostalgia.'

'In France,' said Monsieur Pamplemousse, 'we still do. Wallow, I mean.'

'Would you believe me if I told you I was also Rita Harridge?'

Monsieur Pamplemousse shook his head. He was unprepared for the question. 'She is a writer too?'

'Was,' said Gilbert Beaseley. 'Was. For a while I worked in a joke factory making stick-on phallic symbols for people who can't draw. Then I found employment in a firm of printers. One day I was typesetting a book and I thought to myself "I could do that". That's when Rita first saw the light of day. She had a short life, but a happy one. I think I may say with all due modesty that while she was around Rita caused many a housewife to lay down her feather duster of an afternoon and take to her bed.'

'What happened to her?'

'She had to be put down, poor dear. She was long past her "sell-by" date anyway. Husbands in Ruislip began to

31

complain about the state of their semis. Pity. I think you would have liked her.'

'And your castles which were made of sand?'

'They got washed out to sea, like so much of my life.'

'So what brought you here?' Monsieur Pamplemousse gave an all-embracing wave.

'Ah, well may you ask. I was indulging in my current obsession – a history of Les Baux in the Middle Ages. I thought it would be nice to write a book which didn't dwell on all the carnage over the years: episodes like the well-known after-dinner sport called "Making Prisoners Jump off the Castle Walls and Listening to Their Screams as They Fall to their Death"; that kind of thing. I want to concentrate on the romantic side. The days when the City of Baux was a place of love and played host to trouba-dours and minstrels; when to be accepted, the ladies of the court had to be pretty and high-born. As you may have noticed, I specialise in slim volumes. Alas, if you leave out all the gory bits about Les Baux's past, there isn't a lot left. I've begun to think that Raymond de Turenne, inventor of the jumping game, was on to something. Every time I go up there and see the coach-loads of tourists arriving I think how nice it would be to resurrect it. "Now here we have the very spot where it used to take place. Come a little closer . . . closer still . . ." SHOVE. Posing as a guide you could build up a tidy score in no time at all and no one would be any the wiser.'

'The world,' said Monsieur Pamplemousse, 'is getting vastly overcrowded. The very things people travel miles to see are spoilt before they even get there.'

'How true. Anyway, one day I was doing some research up in the old town when I happened to get into conversa-tion with the producer of this epic at a moment when writers were suddenly thin on the ground. One had gone into a home. Another is reputed to have joined the Foreign Legion. The other three simply walked out and haven't been seen since. On the strength of an old copy of *Sandcastles* I just happened to have with me and a CV I concocted on the spur the moment, he made me an offer I couldn't refuse. *Voilà* . . . here I am.

'I said to him – you'll have to take me as I am. If you don't like what you find, just tell me. I know when I'm not wanted.'

Replenishing his glass, Gilbert Beaseley pushed the bottle across the table. 'I'm talking too much. Tell me about yourself.'

Monsieur Pamplemousse was about to lean forward when he thought better of it. He was also momentarily distracted by the sight of Pommes Frites hurrying back up the slope away from the boat. From the way he kept peering over his shoulder it looked as though he could be in disgrace about something. Guilt was writ large all over his face.

'I am here as a food adviser.'

'A bit late in the day isn't it? I mean, there's only the Last Supper and the Crucifixion to go. No one will get very fat on that, least of all you. There won't even be any leftovers worth speaking of.'

'That is not what I was given to understand.'

Gilbert Beaseley shrugged. 'You may well be right. Things change from minute to minute. The Red Sea was all set to part three days ago – or the Red Sea as represented by a local stretch of water – but it never did. The *Etang de Vaccarès* turned out to be part of the *Réserve Naturelle*. All hell broke loose. They're very hot on conservation down here and no one had got permission to part it.'

Pommes Frites arrived back panting and settled himself under the table. For some reason he was soaked to the skin. Monsieur Pamplemousse also couldn't help noticing there were several small white feathers stuck to his chin.

Gilbert Beaseley glanced down. 'Did you distract the nasty lady, then? Mr Strudel *will* be pleased; so will the crew – they're all on double-time. I only hope you didn't bite her. You could wake up with lock-jaw.'

He turned back to Monsieur Pamplemousse. 'Mrs Noah's being difficult. She has but three lines to say – "Hurry along there", "Two at a time" and "Don't push – there's room for everyone" – not the kind of deathless prose I wish to be remembered by, but at a thousand dollars a word, who's complaining? Besides, in a forty-five-second commercial simplicity is all. Now she's demanding a dialogue coach.'

Monsieur Pamplemousse stared towards the boat. 'Von Strudel is down there?'

'I doubt it. It's the second unit working on some fill-in shots for the Ark sequence.' Beaseley read his thoughts. 'Anyway, I should stay where you are. You'll have plenty of time to see him in action. If you're working on the project there are two things you should know. One: speed is not Von Strudel's middle name. Two: He may be the greatest living authority on biblical films, but to say he is a little out of touch with the stark realities of making television commercials is the understatement of the year. His first shooting script lasted over an hour. That's when they began bringing other writers in, and one by one they have gone – all except for me. He still insists on using his original megaphone.' Beaseley cupped his hands in the shape of a horn. 'Do you vrealise it vas through zis very megundphone zat I called Dietrich *eine Dummkopfe*! If you ask me he's a little bit bonkers.'

'*Comment*?'

'Bonkers. Round the bend. He's been living by himself for too long.'

'Can they not get rid of him?'

'I wouldn't like to be the person who tried. Besides, it would cost too much and the films are vastly over budget as it is. He's getting paid more than the rest of us put together. At his age he doesn't need the money, but he's no fool. Salaries establish the pecking order in this ego-intensive industry. Besides, you know what they say. If you owe someone a thousand dollars you don't sleep at night; make it a million and *they* don't sleep at night. I'll wager Von Strudel sleeps like a log. Apart from that, to fire him would be counter-productive. Time is running out. It could raise all kinds of problems and leave them even worse off.'

'In what way?' Monsieur Pamplemousse was finding it hard to follow the logic.

'The whole thing has to be seen in perspective. This series of commercials may have a bigger budget than *Ben Hur*, but in relation to the potential gross income from the product it is but a drop in the ocean. World-wide we are talking in space-programme terms.'

It occurred to Monsieur Pamplemousse that either he was very low in the pecking order or *Le Guide* must be doing exceptionally well out of him on the quiet. Draining his glass, he made a mental note to tackle the Director on the subject when he had a chance.

'Help yourself,' said Beaseley. 'It's on the house. Von Strudel may be a shit, but at least he's generous with other people's money.'

Monsieur Pamplemousse declined. He was already beginning to feel the effect.

'If it is all so bad, why did you take the job on?'

'A question I ask myself every time I open my eyes in the morning. The sordid truth can be summed up in three words – money, money, money. Also the experience. When it's all over I shall write a book about it. The fact is, ducky, there's more material here than I shall use in a lifetime.'

Gilbert Beaseley looked as though he was about to develop his theme still further but at that moment a loud bang like a pistol shot rang out from somewhere behind them. It was followed by a series of high-pitched bleeps. Monsieur Pamplemousse turned and was just in time to see the gowned figure of a man carrying a large bundle wrapped in a white sheet disappear into one of the trailers. A second loud bang echoed round the clearing as the door slammed shut, but not before he managed to catch a momentary glimpse of a round, whiter than white face surmounted by a mop of curly black hair and behind that, just inside the trailer, a girl whose hair, in striking contrast, was long and ash blonde. She looked as though she was wearing a nurse's uniform.

'*Sapristi!*' He was glad he had resisted the offer of another Ricard. 'Who or what was that?'

'That,' said Gilbert Beaseley, 'was Brother Angelo. The girl is what is euphemistically known as an *au pair* – Swedish version.

'We do sound in a tizz today. It's a good thing he's wearing his bleeper.'

'Brother Angelo?' Monsieur Pamplemousse looked puzzled. 'He is also an adviser?'

Beaseley gazed at him in amazement. 'You must be joking. Don't tell me you've never heard of Brother Angelo? Late of "The Friars" – before he went solo.' He gave a hollow laugh. 'The only thing Brother Angelo could advise anyone on is where to get their next shot of coke. Brother Angelo – whose real name, by the way, is Ron Pickles – is the Pavarotti of the pop world. The one big difference being that Pavarotti doesn't end his act by urinating on an electric guitar. Come to that, neither does Brother Angelo any more. He did it once too often at a concert in Manchester. There was something wrong with the wiring and he received what he fondly calls "a packet up his privates". He could neither let go, nor could he stop peeing. In the end his trousers parted under the strain and a certain HRH who happened to be present complained. Not even his laser-controlled halo could save him from being arrested for indecent exposure. He was lucky not to end up being sent to the Tower.'

'I am afraid I am a little out of touch with the pop world,' said Monsieur Pamplemousse. 'The last concert I

went to was with my wife. Jean Sablon was top of the bill.
"Sur le pont d'Avignon" was all the rage that year.'

'But was it *numéro un*?' said Beaseley.

'I don't think they had numbers in those days,' said
Monsieur Pamplemousse. 'It was done alphabetically.
But it was a very good song. It was on everyone's lips.' He
stared at the closed door of the trailer. 'So what is the
secret of his success?'

'Perfectly simple. Despite everything, our Ron looks
the picture of innocence. Innocence radiates from every
pore. It's that black, curly hair. Women the world over –
that is to say, girls of thirteen plus – all want to mother
him. Mind you, I wouldn't care to be the one who got to
do it. She would be torn limb from limb by the rest of the
mob. In some ways, casting him as Our Saviour was a
stroke of genius, but it is not without its problems.'

'You mean . . . Brother Angelo – Monsieur Pickles – is
playing Christ?' Monsieur Pamplemousse looked aghast
at the thought. 'It is not possible.'

'You could do a lot worse. Can't you just see him in the
part?'

'If you want my opinion,' said Monsieur Pamplemousse, 'the very idea is so grotesque it will offend many
people.'

'Undoubtedly. That's one of the reasons why Von
Strudel was engaged in the first place. There's no such
thing as bad publicity. At least it will get the product
talked about. Strudel has spent his whole life offending
people. His films are monuments to bad taste, but they
are beautifully made. The grammar is immaculate. Nothing tricksy. Long shot, medium shot, close-up. No playing
around with the sound perspective. You always know
exactly where you are.

'Anyway, let's not be stuffy about it. By all accounts
Christ was one of the people, with the power to draw the
multitudes. That describes Ron Pickles down to a tee. It's
the "in" thing – identifying a well-known person with a

perfume. It began in England. The pulling power of Henry Cooper persuaded British men that wearing Brut could be macho; Chanel called on Jack Nicholson when they launched L'Egoïste. They didn't get him, but they called. Besides, who is it going to offend? Not the people who buy XS. They are hardly likely to be offended by anything – and certainly wouldn't admit to it even if they were. Those who might be offended are unlikely to buy it.

'The main trouble lies with Brother Angelo. They have come up against one tiny snag. He suffers from acute coprophalia . . .'

'*Qu'est que c'est*?' Monsieur Pamplemousse's command of English was beginning to desert him. He felt his concentration going.

'Coprophalia? It is an uncontrollable desire to be foul-mouthed. For years he has been totally unable to construct the simplest sentence without using the word "fuck". That may have been all right in the Sheffield steelworks where he first started out, but it doesn't go down too well in the world at large. He's been fitted with a bleeper attached to his voice-box. A kind of early warning system. It is programmed to obliterate certain key words. Luckily the Anglo-Saxons are sadly deficient in the oaths division, so the electronics are comparatively simple. Had our Ron been born in Italy the technical problems would have been immense. It would have needed an entirely new chip. As it is he sometimes sounds like a walking cash register. Fortunately Our Lord was a man of few words and it makes writing the script that much easier.'

'*Excusez-moi*.' Monsieur Pamplemousse reached for the bottle. He suddenly felt in need of a drink.

'Whoever said "you don't have to be crazy in this business, but it helps" knew what he was talking about.' Gilbert Beaseley glanced in the direction of the boat. While they had been talking the lights had been struck and everyone had disappeared. Filming was over for the day. He lifted a wrist and focused on his watch.

'Delightful though it is, I'm afraid we shall have to continue this *conversazióne* some other time. There is an emergency script conference at the Oustau de Baumanière in less than an hour's time.'

'You will not be eating first?' Monsieur Pamplemousse's taste buds were beginning to register the smell of food from somewhere nearby. Pommes Frites was getting the message too. Every now and then he sat up, nose twitching.

'Sadly, no. I may cook myself some sardines on toast later. The muse is calling. Or, to put it another way, I feel it may be expeditious to work on a stand-by script for the Last Supper. Something tells me it should be possible to do better than "someone isn't wearing you-know-what, pause, all but one turn. Cut to BCU of Judas Iscariot. Dissolve." I feel like a schoolmaster, trying to keep one step ahead of his class. I can't stand it when everyone looks at me for an answer and I haven't got one. It makes me feel terribly lonely.

'But as for dinner, far be it from me to tell a food adviser where to eat, but if you take my advice you'll skip the unit caterers, Ratatouilles et Cie. Take advantage of Mr Strudel's absence and dine Chez Montgomery.'

He directed his thumb towards an olive tree some fifty or so metres away, beneath the branches of which a figure in white shorts and a white chef's jacket and *toque* was busying himself over a field kitchen.

'Montgomery is Von Strudel's personal chef. An unlikely name for an Egyptian, but he was born at the time of El Alamein, so he was named after one of our generals.' Beaseley shrugged. 'If things had gone the other way I suppose he would have ended up as Rommel. Only one word of warning. Montgomery is a splendid fellow and he cooks like a dream, but he is given to occasional excesses. Given your problem, I should steer clear of his version of Strawberry Romanov. It goes under

39

the name of *Erdbeeres Von Strudel*. I've heard tell it is positively lethal.'

Gilbert Beaseley paused as he turned to leave. 'Technical question: if comedy is unreal people in real situations, and farce is real people in unreal situations, what do you call unreal people in unreal situations?'

'*Dummkopfs*?'

Beaseley laughed. 'You're learning.'

Monsieur Pamplemousse watched Gilbert Beaseley as he made his way slowly and unsteadily in the direction of his trailer. He had a feeling he had passed some sort of test, but he wasn't sure what.

As the other disappeared from view he rose. Instinct told him to follow Beaseley's advice. No chef likes to be idle. In a profession dedicated to giving pleasure, idleness was like the sounding of a death knell. Never one to miss an opportunity, Pommes Frites followed suit. Although for reasons best known to himself, dinner didn't appear to be high on his list of priorities, it was clear that he, too, recognised the signs.

They were neither of them mistaken.

As the pair of them drew near, Montgomery's face lit up. There followed a burst of frenzied activity. Monsieur Pamplemousse's request for a *pastis* was brushed aside in favour of a kir.

'I make it for you specially. For you I add just a touch of honey. Try it. If you no like, then I will bring you a Ricard.'

The kir arrived at record speed along with a bone for Pommes Frites. Monsieur Pamplemousse tasted the former and murmured his approval, adding that it would perhaps need another to offset the taste of his pastis; in a moment or two – there was no hurry. Seeking Pommes Frites' opinion as to the quality of the bone would have been superfluous. He was managing to force it down.

Moments later a plate of *amuse-gueules* appeared with a flourish: *Caillettes* – tiny meatballs made of pork liver and spinach, flavoured with herbs; and some wafer-thin square slices of toast covered with *Anchoïade* – a combination of anchovies, olive oil, lemon juice and garlic – topped by a slice of fig. The anchovies had been mashed by hand before being blended with the other ingredients and the mixture pressed hard into the toast so that it would absorb the flavour.

After a suitable interval and a second kir, a salad arrived: on a bed of crisp lettuce leaves lay prawns, sliced tomatoes, black olives, *crème fraîche* to which a squeeze of lemon juice and a little basil had been added, mushrooms and asparagus tips. The *vinaigrette* dressing was immaculate. Monsieur Pamplemousse helped himself sparingly to some *aioli* which came in a separate bowl. He doubted if he would be going short of garlic and what was left would keep the flies at bay.

It was a wise move. The monk fish in the *Lotte en Broche* which followed had been marinated with lemon juice and garlic before being interspersed between slices of pepper and onion on skewers fashioned out of rosemary branches. Out of the corner of his eye he'd seen Montgomery basting it every few minutes with a sprig of rosemary dipped in olive oil as it grilled over a charcoal fire. It tasted divine, the rosemary implanting a wonderfully delicate flavour.

The wine was a Côtes de Provence L'Estandon; young and fresh, suitably chilled and in a 'serious' bottle – not one of the traditional fanciful shapes. It was an ideal accompaniment for the spicy food. Fruity, yet with a faint hint of acidity about it.

Rather like Gilbert Beaseley. Beaseley had a touch of acidity. Monsieur Pamplemousse wasn't sure whether he liked him or not. That was probably the way most people felt. He must go through life treating it as an arm's length transaction. Perhaps he'd suffered some great tragedy or disappointment which made him shy of getting too close to people.

The cheese was a *banon*, a small disc-shaped piece covered in chestnut leaves bound with rafia. With it came a glass of red Côtes du Ventoux. The bottle was left on the table. He examined the label. It was from Jean-Pierre Perrin. Once again, a perfect choice. It would accord well with the mildly nutty flavour of the cheese.

Monsieur Pamplemousse sank back into his canvas chair feeling at peace with the world. He didn't envy a soul, not even those who by now would be dining in state at the Oustau de Baumanière. It was a pleasant change to have someone else choose his meal, nicer still not to feel obliged to sit down and write copious notes about it before he retired to bed.

The smell of lavender mingling with that of burning charcoal and rosemary reminded him of the reason for his being there. What a strange world it was, the world of perfume and *haute couture*. XS was a very apt name for one of its products. It summed it all up.

While he had been eating, it had grown dark and lights were twinkling like fireflies around Les Baux. He wondered how Beaseley was getting on. Probably rewriting an abridged version of the Bible. To all intents and purposes it had been written by committee anyway, and then amended down the centuries.

Brother Angelo, too. He hadn't heard or seen a sign of him since his brief appearance. The trailer he'd entered was dark and silent, the curtains tightly drawn.

He wished now that he had asked about Mangetout. From all he had heard she led the life of a recluse these days. Garbo had nothing on her. No doubt Beaseley would fill him in if he asked. It would be something to tell the Director.

'For you, I add a little curaçao.'

A dish of sliced strawberries macerating in orange juice floated before his eyes and he suddenly realised the chef was talking to him.

It was '*Erdbeeres Von Strudel*' time. The combination

of fruit and liqueur seemed overpoweringly heady in the night air. The smell reached out to him and then faded as the dish was whisked away to a nearby table.

'Then . . . a touch of *crème Chantilly*.' The strawberries vanished under a mound of cream.

'Then I add some pepper. Not too little . . . not too much. It is how Herr Strudel likes it.'

Watching Montgomery wielding the giant mill, Monsieur Pamplemousse wondered what would constitute too much. It looked a lethal amount. No wonder Beaseley had warned him against it.

'And then . . . just for you' – Montgomery made his way quickly to the stove, glowing red in the twilight – 'I pass it under the grill . . . like so . . .'

The words had hardly left his mouth when there was a flash like a sheet of lightning. It was followed a split second later by a loud explosion. A cloud of black smoke rapidly enveloped the stove, momentarily obliterating it from view.

Monsieur Pamplemousse picked himself up, but in his haste to see what had happened to Montgomery, who had borne the full brunt of the blast, he tripped over Pommes Frites, lost his balance and landed on the ground again. It was only then, as he gazed up at the back of the chair he had been sitting in a few moments earlier, that he realised whose seat he had appropriated.

Stencilled across the canvas back were the words VON STRUDEL – DIRECTOR (KEEP FOR SERIES).

As he registered the words it occurred to Monsieur Pamplemousse that given Von Strudel's advanced years, had he been performing his party piece that evening, they might well have had cause to replace KEEP FOR SERIES with the letters RIP and yet another chapter in the history of the cinema would have been closed for ever.

3
A STAR IS BORN

'It is good, Herr Strudel, that you have managed to assemble such an agreeable cast.'

Monsieur Pamplemousse hadn't intended using the word *agréable*. It slipped out. He had meant to say *distingué*, but at the last moment he'd wondered whether Von Strudel's French was up to it. So far there had been no indication that it might be. Conversation had been minimal: a one-sided series of guttural grunts.

He could hardly complain, however, at not receiving an immediate reaction to his attempt at breaking the ice.

Reaching for his monocle, Von Strudel screwed it firmly in place over his right eye and glared at Monsieur Pamplemousse as if he had suddenly taken leave of his senses. What was clearly a long-perfected trick of closing his other eye at the same time only served to intensify the effect.

'Zer is no such thing as *ein* actor who is *agréable*,' he barked.

'No actor is *agréable*. Zey are all *Dummkopfs*. Eisenstein vas right. You can do zee same thing *mit eine* dummy. Better! Every one of zem is *ein Dummkopf*.'

Having delivered himself of what he clearly considered to be the final word on the subject, Von Strudel placed the thumb and forefinger of both hands together to form an oblong frame. Peering through the opening, he turned his back on Monsieur Pamplemousse. A squeak which sounded uncannily like two pieces of unlubricated wood rubbing against one another arose as he pivoted on his right leg whilst endeavouring to pan across the pine-clad hills in the far distance.

It was a long pan, for the view from the top of Les Baux afforded an unbroken view of an horizon which seemed to stretch on and on to infinity. Fearful that he might unwittingly be the cause of Von Strudel losing his balance, Monsieur Pamplemousse followed him round.

'Vy do you say zey are *agréable*?'

Monsieur Pamplemousse was rapidly reaching the stage of fervently wishing he'd never mentioned the word. In fact, more than ever he regretted not having postponed delivery of the Director's letter until later in the day. He looked around for a friendly face, but there was no one else in sight. Even Pommes Frites had taken himself off somewhere immediately after breakfast.

Petit déjeuner, taken at a white wooden table beneath a parasol which Montgomery had set up outside his trailer while he was still asleep. It had been a delicious meal. A *petit déjeuner* to be enjoyed at one's leisure and remembered in tranquillity. Closing his eyes while he silently counted up to *dix*, he could still taste it.

Fresh *jus de orange*.

Fromage blanc with cream.

Wild strawberries.

A jug of hot *café*.

Honey and two kinds of *confiture*.

A bowl of cherries.

A wicker basket containing *croissants*, two kinds of toast and a selection of home-made *brioches*.

Beurre.

A white honey-scented buddleia nearby had been alive with bees. Taken in the morning sunshine, they were the ingredients which made it good to be alive. Had such a meal been presented to him at an hotel during the course

of duty, there was no question but that he would have
marked the establishment down as being worthy of three
Stock Pots in *Le Guide*.

And all because he'd been anxious to locate Von
Strudel before work started for the day, he had hurried
over it!

Life was full of regrets. He should have made the most
of his good fortune while it lasted; savoured every mouth-
ful. Given his reception, he was sorely tempted to retrace
his steps down through the old town of Les Baux, where
he had eventually tracked down his quarry, climb into his
car and drive back to base in the hope that he could go
through it all again at a more leisurely pace.

He decided to try another tack. 'I have been doing
some research on the Last Supper, *Monsieur*. Clearly, it
was not an occasion for a banquet. It would have been a
simple meal: some lamb, perhaps, with bitter herbs and
other condiments, a little bread, some wine. There would
have been a bowl of sauce at Our Saviour's side for the
moment when he dipped his bread and handed it to Judas.
It is hard to say what the wine would have been like; most
probably white, possibly sweetish. It would have been
kept in a two-handled clay jar holding nine litres, which
was the official measure at that time, and would then have
been served from a pitcher, which may well have been
decorated. The Romans were fond of such embellish-
ments. Some of them were very elaborate. If you like, I
can show you an illustration of one – it would look very
well on film. Four cups of wine would have been drunk
during the meal to accompany various blessings. To
symbolise the haste with which the Passover meal would
have been eaten at the time of the great escape from
Egypt, the bread would have been unleavened, that is to
say nothing would have been added to produce fermenta-
tion. The lamb would have been roasted . . .'

Monsieur Pamplemousse felt pleased with his dis-
course. He had no idea what message the Director had

conveyed in his letter, but given the limited time available, he felt he hadn't done at all badly in establishing his credentials. Beaseley was right; it was necessary to keep one step ahead of the field.

Von Strudel abandoned his pan in mid flight; Arles and the Grand Rhône were left unexplored. Replacing his monocle, he fixed Monsieur Pamplemousse with a basilisk-like glare. 'Who cares vot zey ate? Actors are not paid to eat. Miming, zey are paid to do. Eatink *nein*.'

Monsieur Pamplemousse tried hard to conceal his disappointment.

'I am afraid I do not understand you, *Monsieur*. The purpose of an adviser, surely, is to advise. If you do not choose to follow the advice, that is your decision. But if such is the case, then I fail to see the purpose of my being here. You do not call in a doctor and then disregard his advice.'

'Advice? Advice? I am surrounded by advice. I cannot even go to the *Badezimmer* without being given advice. I hov advice coming out of *mein Trommelfells*.'

'In that case,' said Monsieur Pamplemousse, 'I will not bother you any further. I am afraid I must ask you to accept my resignation.'

'And I am afraid zat I do not accept it. No vun resigns on zis picture! OK?' Von Strudel glared at him. 'All I vish to know is hov you discovered who is buggink me?'

'*Comment*?'

'Every day since we arrive here somezing goes wrong. Disappearing ink on *mein* script. Toads in *mein* bed. Sand in ze camera vorks. Tyres on *mein* automobile *kaputt*. Now, exploding *Erdbeeres*!' Von Strudel tapped the Director's letter. 'You are here to find ze bugger who is buggink me, is zat not zo, huh?'

'No, zat is not zo,' was the reply which immediately sprang to Monsieur Pamplemousse's mind, but as light slowly began to dawn he paused. He must be getting old. He should have known better. The Director was up to his old tricks again. No wonder the chief had been so anxious to get the meeting in his office over and done with. Just wait!

His silence was misconstrued.

'Zat is good. Now ve know ver ve stand, huh?' Von Strudel beamed *bonhomie*. Exuding brotherly love, he placed an arm round Monsieur Pamplemousse's shoulder.

Monsieur Pamplemousse managed a nod.

'No more of zis talk of resignink?'

With an effort Monsieur Pamplemousse converted the nod into a half-hearted shake. He felt like the victim of some cheap con trick and he didn't as yet trust himself to speak.

'Zat is good,' said Von Strudel. 'Now zat ve understand each other I vill tell you somezing. You are fired!'

The last Monsieur Pamplemousse saw of his erstwhile employer, he was striding purposefully up the hill, peering once again through his makeshift viewer. There was a bang and a whoosh as low-flying air-force jet suddenly shot past without warning, skimming the rooftops. As the noise died away a cry of '*Dummkopf*' echoed round the narrow streets and alleyways of Les Baux.

'Don't take it to heart,' said Gilbert Beaseley. 'Strudel fires people in much the same way as other people offer you a cigarette. He'll have forgotten all about it by the time you next see him. He really should be fitted with a bleeper like Brother Angelo. As for your advice on the catering arrangements at the Last Supper, I shall accept it with gratitude and all due humility.'

He glanced idly at Monsieur Pamplemousse. 'If it's not a rude question, why *did* he fire you? It must be something of a record. Most people manage at least one full day.'

'We had a little misunderstanding.' Monsieur Pamplemousse was reluctant to divulge what had taken place between himself and Von Strudel, least of all to Gilbert

Beaseley, who seemed to thrive on other people's business. He had already said more than he'd intended. Despite everything, and much against his will, he felt himself being drawn into the affair, his appetite well and truly whetted. If he intended taking his mission seriously the least said about it the better. Now that the initial shock of his first encounter with Von Strudel had worn off he had already made up his mind to stay, come what may. 'A confusion of identities, that is all.'

'Conversation with Von Strudel is never easy.' Beaseley took the hint and abruptly changed the subject. 'I heard about last night's kerfuffle. No ill effects, I trust?'

'Some stiffness, that is all. I was sitting far enough away to avoid the blast, and Montgomery managed to roll with the explosion. I saw him at breakfast this morning. Apart from a few strawberry pips embedded in his face, he seemed little the worse for his experience. At some point they will need to be removed.'

'Rumours of sabotage are rife,' said Beaseley. 'It isn't the first thing that's happened. If you ask me, I think someone, for reasons best known to himself, is trying to delay the production.'

'It was more spectacular than lethal. If the speed of the flame which preceded the explosion was anything to go by I suspect some form of *poudre brugère* – the "black powder" which is commonly used in the fireworks industry. Contained, if I am not mistaken, in the pepper pot.'

Beaseley gazed into the middle distance. 'In short, a rather upmarket version of the exploding cigar trick. An interesting theory. Now who on earth would want to do a thing like that? Montgomery wouldn't harm a fly.'

Monsieur Pamplemousse gazed at Gilbert Beaseley speculatively. He sounded genuinely sorry, and yet . . .

On his way back from the abortive meeting with Von Strudel, he had idly straightened the chair he had been sitting in the night before. It was the Capricorn in him. Something made him look under the seat cover and there he'd come across a small rubber cushion. The name of the maker was emblazoned across it: The Whoopie Joke Company, Chicago, Illinois. Relief had been tinged with mortification at being taken in by such a crude joke. He decided to store the information for the time being.

'I doubt if it was meant for Montgomery,' said Monsieur Pamplemousse. 'Apparently it was the first time he had ever made the dish. Normally Von Strudel insists on finishing it off himself. It is his party piece and he is rather proud of it. I suspect Montgomery was a little heavy-handed with the *mouli*.'

Pointedly picking up a copy of a child's version of the Bible he had been reading, he removed a bookmark and opened it at a point where the Easter Story was about to begin. Despite the news that his services as Food Adviser were to all intents and purposes redundant, professional pride made him want to go over the details of the Last Supper one more time.

'Would you care for an up-to-date run-down on today's latest piece of gossip – as at 09.55 this morning?' It was a rhetorical question. Without leaving time for a reply, Gilbert Beaseley pulled up a chair. Monsieur Pamplemousse heaved an inward sigh as he lowered his book again. He gave a non-committal shrug. He had enough on his mind as it was without worrying about the problems of others.

'If you think I am up to it.' He caught sight of some ants on the ground near his feet. One of them was carrying off a breakfast crumb. Relatively speaking it must have weighed a ton; the size of a caber.

'The "Golden Proboscis" has received a nasty letter. It came with this morning's mail.'

'*Le Nez d'Or?*'

'Monsieur Parmentier, *parfumier extraordinaire*; inventor of XS. A rare bird indeed. A man of exquisite taste and possessor of a very unique talent. A man blessed with the ability to remember and identify something in the

51

region of 3,000 different odours. There are only about a dozen others like him in the whole world. Their names never appear on the label, but without them the perfume industry, the top end of it anyway – the part that doesn't rely on chemical substitutes – would collapse overnight.

'I consider myself lucky if I manage to identify one smell at a time. Add brandy and cointreau to my pastis, as is the current ghastly trend, and the old computer in my brainbox goes up in smoke. Utter confusion sets in.'

'What did the note say?'

'The very worst. Some person – or persons – unknown is or are threatening to cut it off.'

'It?'

'His olfactory organ. That organ without which he would be unable to function. Monsieur Parmentier is very unhappy, as well he might be. If I'd spent all those years nurturing my nose, treating it like some rare hothouse plant, keeping it clear of draughts, never going out of my depth in a swimming pool in case the change in pressure affected my sinuses, spraying it morning and night with lightly salted water instead of having a good old-fashioned wash, and then some idiot appeared on the scene threatening to remove it, I'd feel pretty pissed off. It's like having an oil well in your back garden and waking up one morning only to find it's about to run dry.'

'But is he not insured?'

'A very down-to-earth, practical French attitude, if I may say so. Naturally he is insured. But what good does that do anyone? The formula for a perfume is not something you can commit to paper.'

'You mean without Monsieur Parmentier the whole thing would fall apart?'

'His loss would be a disaster. Worse than an opera singer losing his voice. The original formula for XS is a closely guarded secret. Chemical analysis may reveal the basic ingredients, but it won't show how they are put

52

together. Once the current stocks are gone, repeating them will be a major problem. You can't say "take a ton of rose petals or half a ton of this or that, plus a pound of the other". Crops vary for all sorts of reasons; the weather, the time of day when they are picked; Jasmine, for example, needs to be gathered early in the day, ideally before dawn. Ensuring continuity is an art in itself.'

Beaseley broke off as a messenger came roaring up on a scooter and handed him a note. He scanned it briefly, then gave a nod. 'We'll be there.'

'Isn't it delightful,' he remarked to Monsieur Pamplemousse. 'Only in the film business would they call a messenger a gofer – "go for this – go for that . . ." We have received a summons. The "dailies" – yesterday's rushes – are about to be shown.'

'I am included?'

'That's what it says. I told you not to take any notice about getting the sack. Reinstatement is usually swift and painless.'

Monsieur Pamplemousse gave another sigh – audible this time. He marked the place in his book and excused himself while he put it in the trailer for safe keeping.

'It'll be worth going if only to see a minor miracle take place,' called Beaseley. 'I'll wager there won't be a car or a telephone pole or an electric cable or a television aerial in sight. Believe me, that isn't easy. You may think you're out in the wilds, but take a closer look – civilisation is never very far away.'

As they passed Mangetout's trailer they heard the sound of raised voices, interspersed with bleeps.

Beaseley made a face. 'The path of true love never did run smooth. Mangetout doesn't take kindly to the sight of a three-year-old infant mewling and puking in its nurse's arms. The dreaded child has been banished along with Miss Sweden to another caravan. Brother Angelo has taken umbrage. That was the cause of all the fuss yesterday evening.'

'Mangetout and Brother Angelo? But she must be old enough to be his mother.'

'Even worse,' said Beaseley. 'She's the mother of the child.'

Monsieur Pamplemousse stopped in his stride. 'That is not possible.'

'That's probably what they thought at the time. Medically speaking, the odds must have been very much against it. A minor miracle in itself – one for *The Guinness Book of Records*. I looked it up and the last incumbent for the Oldest Mother entry was a Mrs Kistler of Oregon, who was a mere 57+. Brother Angelo and Mangetout aren't exactly in an Abelard and Heloïse situation, but it does make for an interesting subplot in the circumstances. It adds a certain air of incest to the casting. Ron's sponsors would skin him alive if they knew, not to mention the fans. Talking of which, we shall be blessed with several thousand of them over the next few days.'

'They are being allowed in?'

'It's one of Von Strudel's happier thoughts. In some ways it is a stroke of genius. Having Brother Angelo play the lead means Von Strudel has immediate access to his fan clubs and as many extras as he needs. Tomorrow they descend on us ready to line the streets of Les Baux for the filming of the Crucifixion. They would probably carry out the deed for free as well if they knew the truth.'

'All for the sake of a bottle of XS!'

'All for the sake of a bottle of XS. I'll tell you something else about the perfume business. On the one hand it is a very precise science and on the other hand it is an extraordinary hit and miss affair. Enormous risks are taken. Rumour has it that when XS was first presented it was one of some thirty samples. The owner of the company – he whose name on a product causes women's hearts to beat faster and men to reach for their wallets – blanched at the sight of so many bottles laid out before him. He could have cried out *Sacré bleu*! or even *Nom d'un nom*, but instead he threw up his hands, pointed vaguely in the direction of the twenty-third bottle, and uttered the immortal words *c'est excessive*! Which is how it got its name.'

'Do you believe that?'

'It's a nice story – the kind of story you *want* to believe. Repeated often enough – and it will be if the Press Office are doing their stuff – it will become true.

'Anyway, it's in the best Coco Chanel tradition. She is reputed to have chosen No. 5 out of ten sample perfumes because it happened to be her lucky number. She lived on the royalties until the day she died.'

As they reached the viewing theatre, Gilbert Beaseley ushered Monsieur Pamplemousse up some steps and into a large air-conditioned room. Some ten or a dozen velvet-covered armchair seats faced an uncurtained screen on either side of which were two enormous loud-speakers. At the back of the room there was a small sound console and behind that a projection booth. There was a cabinet in one corner on top of which stood an espresso coffee machine and a jug of iced water. The walls were lined with velvet drapes. The ceiling was faced with non-reflecting material and there was thick carpet under-foot. Not surprisingly, voices sounded muted. More than half of the seats were already occupied and Beaseley performed the introductions.

There was hollow laughter when Monsieur Pample-mousse gave the official reason for his presence. An American sound engineer suggested he might start by advising the unit caterers. The second unit director echoed his agreement.

'When I leave here I'm gonna have *ratatouille* with-drawal symptoms.'

The subject of Monsieur Parmentier's letter came up. Various theories were propounded. Anne-Marie, the key make-up artist – dark, green-eyed and unmistakably

French – suggested it might be the work of a rival perfume company. Láslo, the Hungarian art director, threw up the thought that it might be one of the local growers who'd been done out of a contract. More and more distilleries were turning to the Middle East for their flower crops. The French director of photography, Jean-Paul, was convinced it was the work of a religious group – possibly Christian fundamentalists. The continuity girl – who could have been German – disagreed. It was the Jews. In a matter of moments a multilingual argument was in full spate.

Beaseley led the way to two vacant seats at the back of the room.

'All this is a bit of a waste of time,' he murmured. 'They're giving up on the Ark. I managed to talk them out of it last night.'

Monsieur Pamplemousse glanced at his companion with renewed respect. There must be more to him than he'd imagined.

'Have you ever thought about it?' Beaseley went on. 'I mean – *really* thought about it? What the Ark must have been like. All those animals packed in one small boat, crapping and fornicating all over the place. It's the last setting I'd choose for a perfume advert. You can hardly repeat the "Someone isn't using XS" gag.'

The buzz of conversation died down as Von Strudel entered with his 'fixer' and took his seat in the front row.

'I am ready for ze *Bildmusters*,' he announced.

The fixer clicked his fingers and an unseen hand dimmed the lights.

A leader appeared on the screen followed by a shot of the clapper board. The name of the production, the director and the cameraman filled the top half. The scene and take number were chalked on the bottom section.

'Has anyone thought,' whispered Monsieur Pamplemousse, 'that XS wouldn't even have existed in those days. Distillation wasn't invented until the tenth century.'

'Ssh!' Beaseley put a finger to his lips as the hinged

clapper stick came down with a sharp crack, providing a start mark for sound synchronisation. 'You'll do us all out of a job. Ours is not to reason why. Ours but to carry out such crumbs of ideas as the agency people throw at us.'

'So why are we bothering to watch?'

'Questions. Questions. Quite honestly, I don't know. There are moments in life when it's easier to toe the party line.'

Monsieur Pamplemousse sank back into his seat and watched while a succession of shots, each with its separate number, came and went. Water from a rain machine started up. There were shots of the Ark's prow. Shots of the stern. Shots of the gangway. Close-ups of Noah and his wife. Their three sons and their wives were nowhere to be seen. Retake followed retake. The reasons multiplied. Fluffed lines. Passing aircraft. A flock of birds when there should only have been two. There was enough film to make fifty commercials. The sky grew darker and all the time the rain came down, unremitting in its intensity. Whatever else one might say about Mrs Noah, she was certainly earning her money in one respect. She looked soaked to the skin.

'What about the animals?' whispered Monsieur Pamplemousse.

He felt Beaseley's pitying glance. 'This is the cinema. The quickness of the cut deceives the eye. The animals are all over the world. Cairo, Washington, Tokyo – you name it. They get edited in later. Only the Ark is here and that, as we all know, has its problems. Imagine what it would be like if you had animals too.'

'And the doves?'

'They belong to one of Jean-Paul's many cousins.'

'Of course,' said Monsieur Pamplemousse, drily.

'*Halt!*'

'Hold it!' The fixer, whose sole function appeared to be that of acting as Von Strudel's shadow, repeating his words and translating them when necessary into an understandable language, echoed the command.

'*Merde!*' Jean-Paul's voice came out of the darkness. 'I said to lose that shot.'

The editor apologised.

'We're coming to the end anyway,' said the second unit director. 'That's when we ran out of doves. Remember? Fifteen Goddamn doves and they all disappeared!'

Monsieur Pamplemousse, who had been contemplating trying to catch up on some lost sleep, sat up, the memory of the look on Pommes Frites' face the night before still fresh in his mind: the look, the feathers. It was no wonder he hadn't seemed particularly hungry.

'*Umrollen.*'

'Roll back.'

He sank back into his seat as a familiar image filled the screen. Caught during a break in the filming, Pommes Frites was standing on three legs gazing in astonishment at something just out of frame to his right. As the camera zoomed back to a wider angle, a palm tree which had been lying on the ground a short distance away, pivoted on its base until it was in vertical juxtaposition with the principal subject. Through the magic of reverse projection the reason for Pommes Frites' stance became clear, as a stream of water emerged from the tree and made its way rapidly back to source. The action completed, Pommes Frites replaced his nearside rear leg on the ground and backed out of shot.

'*Halt!*'

'Hold it!'

'*Vroll!*'

'Roll!'

Pommes Frites re-entered the picture, eyed the palm tree for a brief moment, then lifted his leg and stood contemplating his immediate surroundings while he obeyed the call of nature. As the tree began to topple over he did a double-take. The camera zoomed in again to show him registering a mixture of alarm and disbelief.

'So much for *papier-mâché* trees,' said someone. 'They'll never replace the real thing.'

Láslo, the designer, gave a groan.

'Not a very good advert for the local water,' murmured Beaseley. 'It confirms my faith in Ricard.'

They watched as Pommes Frites continued on his way. Recovering from the shock, he gave the fallen tree a tentative sniff. Then, having ignored what was obviously a genuine almond tree in favour of conserving his supplies for another occasion, he headed towards the Ark. Whether by accident or design, he was halfway up the gangway when the rain machine started up again.

'*Halt!*'

'Hold it!'

'*Beleuchten!*'

'Lights!'

A large digital clock above the screen showed that from beginning to end the whole sequence had lasted no more than a minute and a half, but during that time Pommes Frites had run the gamut of his emotions. Dignity in repose had given way to alarm and bewilderment. Guilt became friendly interest, then on an instant changed to shock as the rain came down. Disappointment and disgust with mankind in general had permeated his visage as he made his final exit down the gangplank. It was Lewis Milestone's Judge Hardy combined with the natural elegance of Ronald Colman. It was Olivier at Agincourt. At moments it recalled both Edward G. Robinson and W. C. Fields. Edward Everitt Horton sprang to mind; there were shades of Walter Matthau.

Only reproach and a desire for revenge were absent from his face, neither qualities being part of Pommes Frites' make-up, but by the time he had disappeared from view the house lights were on and Von Strudel was addressing the others.

'I vant zat *hund*.'

'But . . .'

'No buts . . . Zat *hund* has star quality. I vant him in ze picture. Zat *hund* is *ein* genius.

'So ve write him in, huh?' He glared across the room at someone who'd had the temerity to point out a basic problem with his thinking.

'Here we go again.' Beaseley looked gloomy. 'I knew it was all too easy. Never write for films. It's like throwing your nearest and dearest to the wolves. If you don't like watching your brain child being butchered first thing every day, forget it.'

An argument broke out near the front over the ethics of using a dog in a biblical scene.

'Wait till the network committees back in the States get to see it!'

'It'll be hacked to pieces.'

'You won't even have to go that far. How about the agency?'

Von Strudel's voice overrode them all.

'Who says Christ did not have *ein* dog? Ver is it written in the Bible that Christ did not have *ein* dog? Show me ver it is vritten. Zat *hund* vill provide the missing link. He vill bind ze whole thing together. Ve vill have him appear in every episode. Zer vill be continuity.'

'Bloodhounds weren't around then.' It was clutching at straws time on someone's part.

'Send him to make-up. Tell them ze problem. By the time zey have finished with him no one vill know him from *ein Wiener Schnitzel*.

'Vat is his name? Ver can we contact him?'

'His name is Pommes Frites!' Monsieur Pamplemousse felt it was high time he made a contribution, however slight.

'That'll have to be changed.' The fixer added his mite to the argument. 'You know what that means in America? French fries. That's something you get on the side.'

'Who cares what he's called?' said a voice. 'It's a commercial. There won't be any credits.'

'What about when he goes up for his awards?' It was hard to tell whether or not Láslo was being serious. Monsieur Pamplemousse suspected not.

'What awards?'

'Who knows? He could get his paw-mark in the cement outside Grauman's. You can't say it was made by a Pommes Frites.'

'Think of Lassie.' It was the second unit director. 'Lassie started off as a Laddie and before that he was called Pal.'

'How about Pommes Nouvelles?'

'Or Duchesse? It doesn't have to be a he.'

'In that case, how about Dauphine? Dauphine would be great.'

'Does he have a ten percenter?'

'*Ja*! Ver is his agent?' Von Strudel gazed around the room.

'I think he means you,' murmured Beaseley. 'Now's your big moment.'

Monsieur Pamplemousse rose to his feet. 'I think there is something you should all know,' he said. 'I am not, as it happens, Pommes Frites' agent. He is perfectly capable of looking after himself. But I think I know him sufficiently well to speak on his behalf and to say that under no circumstances would he agree to changing his name – let alone his sex. As for his appearing in a film advertising perfume, that is up to him. He may or may not agree to it. If he does not want to take part, then nothing on earth will persuade him otherwise. If you wish to contact me in order to discuss the matter further, you will find me in my quarters. I am at your disposal.'

Utter silence prevailed as Monsieur Pamplemousse made his way towards the exit. As he closed the door behind him he heard Von Strudel's voice.

'Who vas that person? Ver have I seen zat man before? Vy does he keep buggingk me?'

Back in his trailer, Monsieur Pamplemousse picked up

61

the telephone and dialled his office number. He was put
through to the Director's office straight away.

'Monsieur Pamplemousse? It is Véronique. *Comment
ça va?*

'*Non, Monsieur* . . . the Director is not here. He left a
little while ago for an unknown destination . . . *Oui, une
destination inconnue* . . .

'*Non, Monsieur* . . . he did not even tell me . . .'

There was a pause. 'Monsieur Pamplemousse . . .'

'*Oui*, Véronique?'

'Perhaps I should not say this, but before he left he sent
out for a bottle of *huile de soleil* – a large one – and he
took with him a case containing his summer clothes. I
think it is possible he may be heading south.'

'Aah! Ah, I see.' Monsieur Pamplemousse thanked the
Director's secretary and then replaced the receiver.

He picked up his book and removed the marker. It was
the beginning of Jesus' last week on earth. He was about
to set out with his disciples on their pre-ordained journey
to Jerusalem.

Without being in the slightest bit blasphemous and on a
totally different level, Monsieur Pamplemousse couldn't
help but sense a parallel in his own life. The news that
Monsieur le Directeur had set out from Paris for an
unknown destination had more than a touch of inevitability about it too.

It was after midday – Jesus had just acquired a donkey
and her foal in Bethfage – when Monsieur Pamplemousse
happened to glance up from his book, distracted by
movement outside his window. Halfway between his own
quarters and those of Mangetout a man in blue overalls
was screwing a name board on to the door of one the
spare trailers he'd noticed the previous evening.

Opening *Le Guide's* issue case, he removed the Leitz
Trinovid binoculars and directed them towards the board.
As the man stood back to admire his handiwork, the

words POMMES FRITZ swam into sharp focus. So Von Strudel had got his way after all: willingly or unwillingly, Pommes Frites was setting out on the road to stardom, nobbled while his master's back was turned, and was exchanging his usual sleeping accommodation on the floor for a bed of his own. And he had succeeded in keeping his own name – more or less.

Monsieur Pamplemousse lowered his glasses. He was about to reach for the telephone handset when he hesitated. The whole thing was utterly ridiculous. Talented though he undoubtedly was, there were some things beyond even Pommes Frites' capabilities. Answering the telephone was one of them.

What was it Beaseley had said? 'You don't have to be crazy to work in films, but it helps'? Clearly, as a disease, it was catching.

On the other hand – he checked Pommes Frites' number against a plan on the wall, then reached for the telephone again – on the other hand, it was tough at the top and already Pommes Frites could be feeling a trifle lonely, wondering perhaps if he had made the right decision. A single ring might well provide a much-needed crumb of comfort; a sign that someone, somewhere, was thinking of him.

4
THE LAST SUPPER

They began to arrive in the late afternoon of the day before the shooting of the Crucifixion; by van, by car and on foot. Some were dressed in shorts and sleeveless tops, others in factory-frayed, cut-off jeans and T-shirts bearing the motto 'Brotherly Love' stencilled below a picture of their hero.

The more enterprising, aware of the fact that they would be paid extra if they came in costume, wore the dress of the period. The women were mostly clad in long, plain black or dark-blue gowns, with a wide leather girdle round the waist. They wore a square piece of folded cloth of the same colour on their head, either hanging down behind or used as a turban. Others wore plain, homespun woollen dresses, relieved by coloured handwork at the neck.

Some of the men – who were mostly older and in the minority – wore loincloths, often supporting a *bedon* which was far from *petit*; many were bearded, and almost all wore thonged leather sandals. The more adventurous sported priestly robes of blue-edged purple over linen breeches and undershirt. The tinkling of bells as they walked could be clearly heard across the valley.

They converged as if by common consent on an area just outside the perimeter of the location site. Tents were erected. Smoke began to rise from camp fires. It was like a remake of the trek to the Promised Land.

Using a borrowed lighting stand as a support, Monsieur Pamplemousse set up his Leica and began shooting off a reel of FP4. With the mountains in the background and the smoke and the Brueghel-like wandering figures it cried out for black and white. It would make a good illustration for an article in *Le Guide*'s staff magazine. Calvet, the editor of *L'Escargot*, might welcome it as a change from Guilot's endless articles on hiking or one of Bernard's treatises on the cultivation of the rose.

'Setting up in opposition?' Beaseley materialised beside him, smelling of pastis and after-shave.

'Hardly.'

'It's quite a sight. Rather awe-inspiring in a way.'

'It would be interesting to know what motivates them.' Monsieur Pamplemousse moved his makeshift tripod a little to the left and changed the lens to a narrow angle.

'Word gets around,' said Beaseley. 'It's something to focus their energies on. All the same, some of them must have travelled thousands of miles to be here. I can't see myself doing it. It makes me feel old.'

'Don't tell me,' said Monsieur Pamplemousse wrily. 'Policemen are starting to look younger.'

'Chief constables are starting to look younger,' said Beaseley gloomily.

Monsieur Pamplemousse glanced at him. 'With respect, you are no longer seventeen.'

'Neither are a good many of that lot,' said Beaseley. 'Take away the teeny-boppers and the average age is higher than you'd think.'

'Perhaps,' said Monsieur Pamplemousse simply, 'Brother Angelo is blessed with that mysterious ingredient known as "star" quality. It is a God-given attribute. You either have it or you don't.'

'I suppose that's why he got the part.' After his exposition of the night before Beaseley sounded less sure of himself, as though he were having second thoughts.

'You're right, though. Whatever it is, our Ron's got more than his fair share. I happen to know from the person who looks after his fan mail that all over the world – from Winnipeg to Wellington, from Florence to Folkestone – there are women awaiting his call. They have a bag packed and stashed away under the bed ready to leave home at a moment's notice.'

'That is true?'

'It's not only true, but I have a feeling my informant wouldn't mind dropping everything herself if the chance arose.'

'Some people need to live out their fantasies with a person who, deep down, they know will never be theirs,' said Monsieur Pamplemousse. 'It avoids the moment of truth.'

'I wouldn't go so far as to say that,' said Beaseley. 'By all accounts Ron has done his bit towards making other people's fantasies come true. Whenever he gives a concert he hands his manager a list of the ones in the front row he'd like to stay behind. Most of them are only too happy to oblige. Who knows what exposure to hot Provençal nights will do to some of those out there. There have already been several attempts at breaking into the site just to be near him and it isn't even dark yet. I fear the worst.'

Monsieur Pamplemousse listened with only half an ear. He was concentrating instead on trying to take a picture with the minimum number of vehicles in shot. It wasn't easy. More were arriving every minute. Even as he checked the focus on what he thought would be his final shot, a car rather larger and more opulent-looking than the rest entered the frame. It disappeared momentarily behind an outcrop of rocks, then came to an abrupt halt as it emerged on the other side and came up against a veritable wall of human bodies, completely ruining his composition.

It was a Citroën DX25. A black Citroën DX25.

Monsieur Pamplemousse's heart sank as he watched

the driver climb out of the car and, after engaging some of
the crowd in conversation, turn and begin heading in the
direction of the location, signing autographs as he went.
The mannerisms, the walk, the air of authority were all
too familiar.

'Is anything wrong?' asked Beaseley.

Monsieur Pamplemousse pressed the shutter for luck.
'Not really. It is just someone I would rather not see.'

'Ah, the world is full of those,' said Beaseley sympa-
thetically. 'Talking of which reminds me of Von Strudel.
We have just been locked in mortal combat. The good
news is I may never be asked to work on a film script
again.'

'It is that serious?' Monsieur Pamplemousse reloaded
his camera and then started packing up the equipment,
slotting the various items into their allotted places in the
tray which was part of *Le Guide*'s issue case. He couldn't
help but feel rather more concerned about his own affairs
than Beaseley's. It was bad news if the Director had taken
it into his head to pay him a visit. Any hopes of a quiet
few days would be gone. He should have realised what
was afoot from his telephone conversation with Véronique.

He forced himself to return to his companion. 'Did you
get the menu for the Last Supper? I asked the gofer to
make sure it reached you before work started.'

'I did, thank you very much,' said Beaseley. 'Apart
from the lamb – I feel it is a moot point as to whether it
would have been roasted or boiled – I couldn't fault it.
However, I'm afraid that's where the trouble started. It
seems that Mangetout is a Vegan.'

'Mangetout?' Monsieur Pamplemousse came down to
earth with a bump. 'But surely the Virgin Mary wasn't
present at the Last Supper?'

'My words exactly,' said Beaseley. 'That was when I ran
foul of her agent – an American gentleman from one of
the less salubrious areas of New York. He has never

68

learned the meaning of the word "No"; although, in fairness, I suppose that's what makes him a good agent.

'You know what he said? "That's her boy up there. You think she's going to let him be all alone on his last night?"

'Picture the scene,' continued Beaseley. 'A patch of hilly ground in the Camargue. A crowd of people are gathered round a room which, for practical reasons, has only three sides made out of canvas and plywood to resemble a house in Jerusalem circa AD30. The fourth side is peopled by some of the highest paid technicians in the world, all set to go. They have the benefit of the greatest lighting engineer in the business overhead, but filming being a belt and braces operation, arc lights are standing by at the ready lest He should take umbrage, as well He might when He hears what's going on down below. The Heavens could grow dark.

'Seeing that something was expected of me, I made what I still think is a valid point.

' "How," I asked, "does she know it's his last night?" Do you know what the answer was?'

Monsieur Pamplemousse shook his head.

' "It ain't negotiable. It's in her contract. Where he goes – she goes." It seems Mangetout is insisting on having her part built up. Short of having her say things like "watch out – the plates are hot," or "Anyone for mint sauce?" I'm afraid my mind went a total blank on the subject. "If that's the way it is," I said to her agent, "why don't you play the one who isn't wearing XS? You can be Judas and all the other agents can be the rest of the disciples – then everyone will be happy." As a suggestion it went down like a lead balloon.'

'But the whole thing is monstrous. *Incroyable*. It is little short of *sacrilège*.'

'I take heart,' said Beaseley, 'with something the editor whispered to me as I made my exit. "There's always the cutting-room floor." The whole episode, from the opening establishing shot until the villain of the piece, Judas Iscariot, is revealed, lasts less than a minute. The cameraman's no happier than I am – he's having to shoot Mangetout through gauze.'

'What did Brother Angelo have to say about it all?'

' "****ing ****!" I quote. Then he buried his head in his hands. Which sums up my feelings too. I have an idea that particular clause in Mangetout's contract wasn't of his making, nor that of his own agent.

'Come,' Beaseley beckoned to Monsieur Pample-mousse. 'I suggest we take a little stroll in the general direction of Jerusalem and you can see for yourself. Unless, of course, you want to stay and see your friend.'

Monsieur Pamplemousse's moment of hesitation was but a token gesture. 'I shall be happy to join you. If I stay I may end up saying something I regret.'

'Heaven forbid!' said Beaseley. 'Follow me. But don't say I didn't warn you.'

Monsieur Pamplemousse and Beaseley arrived on the set during a break in filming. Jesus and his disciples were seated round a long table in what purported to be the upper room of a house. The beginnings of a mock staircase to what would normally have been the stables in the room below led nowhere. At the head of the table, Brother Angelo was hardly recognisable with his moustache and beard. Mangetout stood a little behind him, but just out of shot, holding a dish of lamb. She looked decidedly unhappy.

It was all much as Beaseley had described it: Rome might not have been built in a day, but a very passable replica of a street in old Jerusalem had been constructed overnight. Façades of houses were supported from behind by scenery props kept in place by weights and sandbags. Scaffolding held up the Palace of the High Priest, Caiaphas, which towered above everything else. Giant white screens reflected the sunlight on to the set, filling in the shadows. Cables snaked in every direction.

As with all film sets, technicians and hangers-on seemed to outnumber the actors by something like ten to one. Each had their part to play; all were ready to do their bit at a moment's notice.

The make-up girl Monsieur Pamplemousse had seen during the screening of the rushes – Anne-Marie – darted in with a palette-shaped board and some brushes. She dabbed Brother Angelo's brow dry of sweat, repaired the damage with a dusting of powder, automatically removed a strand of hair from his shoulder, then darted off again. A male dresser wielding a clothes brush looked put out. A demarcation line had been crossed.

Monsieur Pamplemousse couldn't help but notice that Mangetout looked more than put out. Perhaps other demarcation lines had been crossed as well?

Beaseley noticed it too. 'I wouldn't like to be in Ron's shoes,' he murmured. 'I bet he doesn't get "Happiness Is . . ." sung to him over breakfast. She's jealous as hell of anything in skirts that moves.'

Someone called for quiet.

Monsieur Pamplemousse glanced around for Pommes Frites and spotted him with his wrangler in a mock-up stable area near to where Mangetout was standing. Half hidden by a lamp, he was probably waiting for a cue. One thing was certain – if he hadn't yet had lunch he must be feeling hungry.

The cameraman climbed aboard his dolly and the sound engineer racked out the microphone, swinging it up and down, testing for shadows.

'I thought the Last Supper took place after dark,' whispered Monsieur Pamplemousse.

'It will by the time they've finished with it,' said Beaseley. 'Day for night filming. Filters.' He put a finger to his lips.

Von Strudel was sitting nearby, a green eye-shield pulled down over his brow, his wooden leg resting on

71

another chair. It was hard to tell if he was awake or not. He raised his right hand.

'Roll camera.' His fixer translated the signal into words.

After a few seconds the camera operator called 'Speed.'

'Mark it.'

The clapper boy ran in front of the lens and held up his board.

'Scene twenty-three. Take seven.'

'Action.'

As the camera started to dolly in there was the distant drone of an approaching aeroplane.

'*Scnitt*!' Von Strudel raised his left hand.

'Cut!' The fixer echoed his command.

Von Strudel glared up at the sky. He placed the megaphone to his lips. '*Dummkopf*!'

Everyone waited patiently for the plane to pass. When all was quiet the whole procedure began again.

'Roll camera.'

'Speed.'

'Mark it.'

The clapper boy ran on. 'Scene twenty-three. Take eight.'

'Action.'

The camera began to dolly in once again for the opening establishing shot and then stopped. The sun had moved and there was a shadow which hadn't been there before. In trying to avoid it the camera operator was shooting off. There was also a troublesome reflection.

After a brief discussion with the director of photography, the set designer had a word with the unit manager. A carpenter appeared and added a strip of plywood to one side of the third wall. A scenic artist carrying a giant pot and a huge brush followed in his wake, splashing paint around with an air of abandon. In a moment the wood was transformed into stone. It looked as though the rocks had been there for ever.

Jean-Paul called for someone to 'Chinese' a barn door. The lighting gaffer called across to the best boy, who reached up with a pole and knocked the metal covering of a lamp through ninety degrees so that a vertical strip of light became horizontal. It was another world, and like all other worlds it had its own language. It would have been hard to justify the arrangement to a time and motion study person, but then time and motion people didn't make films.

Someone else ambled on to the set and sprayed a dish with dulling liquid.

The camera operator announced there was a hair in the gate. He climbed off the dolly and began removing a large soundproofing blimp covering the camera. The focus puller seized the opportunity to reload the film.

'All right, everyone. Take five.'

A buzz of conversation went up all around as those who weren't involved relaxed. Mangetout put her plate down on a stool near Brother Angelo and passed a comment. He gave a shrug and she retired into the shadows. It was easy to see why. Daylight didn't lend enchantment.

The wrangler said something to Pommes Frites, then left him to his own devices. Pommes Frites hesitated for a moment before settling down to await his next instructions. He was wearing his enigmatic expression and it was impossible to tell what, if anything, he was thinking. Monsieur Pamplemousse would have given a lot to know, but Pommes Frites seemed to be studiously avoiding his gaze – whether out of pique or guilt it was impossible to say, and before he had a chance to make the first move Beaseley took hold of his arm.

'Feel like a stroll?'

'*Une bonne idée.*'

They walked in silence for a while, picking their way in and out of the cables and equipment and groups of extras taking time off for a quick smoke.

'What gave them the idea?' asked Monsieur

Pamplemousse idly as they finally reached open ground.

'You mean the Last Supper?'

'Not only that – the whole thing – using scenes from the Bible to sell perfume.'

'Don't ask me. I came in halfway through. I suppose it hasn't been done before. It's the ultimate. It has every-thing. Someone once said there are only six plots in the world and they are all in the Old Testament. Follow that, as they say.'

'But someone must have suggested it in the first place,' persisted Monsieur Pamplemousse.

'Who knows where ideas spring from?' said Beaseley. 'Normally it would start with the agency. A company entrusts itself to one of the big boys and relies on them to come up with ideas. Why do you ask?'

Monsieur Pamplemousse didn't really know. It was simply a little nagging question in the back of his mind. A tiny voice.

'It seems to have upset a lot of people.'

'You mean all the sniping that's been going on?'

Sniping was one way of putting it. Monsieur Pample-mousse felt he would have used a stronger word. Some-one was trying to make a point and the method of doing it ranged from schoolboy practical jokes to verging on the deadly serious. So far no one had been injured, but there was always a first time. As far as he could make out there was a list as long as his arm of people who had it in for Von Strudel. Or, if not for Von Strudel himself, for those he represented. It was strange that so far no one had claimed responsibility.

'There must be simpler ways of making a commercial. Less likely to offend. Less costly.'

'We are talking films,' said Beaseley. 'Films, perfume and advertising – a lethal combination. Cost doesn't enter into it. I'll give you an example. Chanel never give out figures, but when they launched Egoïste Jean-Paul Goude was commissioned to make a thirty-second commercial featuring the Carlton Hotel in Cannes. He had a mock-up of it built in Brazil, flew everyone out there and took ten days over the shooting. The cost must have been horrendous. You might ask, why Brazil? Answer: because the Director decided the light was better.'

'And was it?'

'Possibly.'

'Would anyone have noticed the difference?'

'I doubt it. But the publicity which followed was worth its weight in gold. And that was nothing compared to this. The column inches already written about XS would stretch from here to Grasse and back. Come up and see me some time and I'll show you my press cuttings.'

Beaseley caught the sidelong glance Monsieur Pamplemousse gave him.

'I was only joking,' he said hastily. 'The point I'm trying to make is that advertising is the stuff that dreams are made of – to misquote William Shakespeare. The life it pretends to portray doesn't, couldn't and probably should never exist. In my view it is responsible for a great many of the ills of this world, for it makes people restless for the so-called "better life". In that respect it offers up much the same thing as Brother Angelo, and there is about the same chance of achieving it.'

'It seems to me,' said Monsieur Pamplemousse, 'that a great many people would envy Brother Angelo.'

'Brother Angelo, perhaps,' said Beaseley. 'But is Ron Pickles happy? Not from all I've seen.

'As for choosing something simple, simple ideas are the hardest of all to come by. Anyway, it isn't such a bad notion. It's going back to basics. The Romans were into perfume in a big way. What did the Three Wise Men take with them as gifts when they visited Bethlehem after Jesus was born? Gold, frankincense and myrrh. Two out of three can't be bad. If Von Strudel had his way he would skip the gold and show them taking a bottle of XS as well. It's lucky no one's thought of it.'

75

'Mangetout is hardly my idea of the Virgin Mary,' said Monsieur Pamplemousse. 'Seen close to she is something of a disappointment.'

'Ravaged is the word,' said Beaseley. 'I agree it isn't exactly type-casting, but we all see things in our own way. With great respect to your lovely country and your good self, I suppose I've always seen Virgin Mary as being rather English – probably born somewhere near Guildford. In much the same way as I've always pictured Christ being British. A bit chauvinistic really. I daresay you people think he was French.'

'Naturellement,' said Monsieur Pamplemousse drily.

'Exactly. You could say that in choosing someone as unlikely as Mangetout nobody gets really upset because they know it isn't definitive and it still leaves them with their options open. Our heroine is mean, moody, magnificent and available – always has been. Did you know her real name is Haricot? Mangetout is much more apt. She devours anyone who comes near. I'm told that at one period in her career – when she was "resting" – she was known as Madame Flageolet.'

'And yet she decided to have Brother Angelo's baby.'

'Rcn power,' said Beaseley. 'She knows he'd be off like a shot otherwise and she probably needs his money to keep her in the style to which she has become more than accustomed.'

As they arrived back on the set they heard Von Strudel's voice raised in anger. An argument appeared to be in progress between him and Brother Angelo.

'This bread,' said Brother Angelo, 'is ****ing awful. It tastes like ****. There's something ****ing wrong with it.'

Von Strudel raised the megaphone to his lips. 'You vill eat it und like it,' he bellowed. 'Zis is your chosen profession.'

'No it ****ing isn't!' Brother Angelo sounded equally

incensed. 'And don't ****ing shout at me. I'm not ****ing deaf.'

Clearly an impasse had been reached. How long it would have gone on for or what possible solution might have been arrived at, was hard to say, but attention was suddenly diverted by a cry from Mangetout.

'*Merde!*'

She held aloft an empty serving dish.

'*Le chien!*'

The delivery of the words *le chien* was on a par with the celebrated mouthing by Dame Edith Evans of the phrase 'a handbag' in *The Importance of Being Ernest*, but there the similarity ended. It was followed by a stream of invective which would have blown the fuses on Brother Angelo's bleeper had he been given the lines to say.

Gradually, as Mangetout's anger subsided, those around became aware of some singularly unpleasant noises coming from somewhere outside their line of vision. The cause became clear almost immediately as Pommes Frites tottered into view, his head held low, his legs looking as though they might give way at any moment. The sight of the empty plate in Mangetout's hand gave rise to fresh paroxysms. Unhappiness rubbed shoulders with both guilt and regret as he averted his gaze.

'The *lamm*,' shouted Von Strudel. 'Somevun has poisoned ze *lamm!*'

Brother Angelo gazed triumphantly round the assembly.

'What did I ****ing tell you?' he cried. 'It takes a ****ing dog to show you who's ****ing right. Now, do you ****ing believe me.'

Despite the glowing testimonial from such an unexpected source, Pommes Frites had the grace to look ashamed of himself as he made a beeline for the nearest bush and began another bout of retching.

It was difficult in the circumstances not to feel slightly holier than thou.

'The Lord giveth,' said Beaseley, 'and He taketh away. I'm glad I'm not a wrangler. I think there's some clearing up to be done.'

Having seen Pommes Frites safely to the unit vet's quarters at the other end of the location, Monsieur Pamplemousse made his way slowly back to his quarters.

Animal-like, Pommes Frites was already looking little the worse for his experience, but there was no sense in taking chances. The vet was English and a man of few words. He promised to keep Monsieur Pamplemousse informed if there was any change for the worse. Otherwise . . . a shrug indicated that he shared Pommes Frites' views on such matters. A few blades of grass would probably work wonders – were there any grass to be found. The patient would soon be back on solids. In the meantime he would keep him under observation.

Back in his trailer, Monsieur Pamplemousse decided it was time for *déjeuner*. He examined the contents of his refrigerator, and after a moment's thought removed four eggs and broke them into a bowl. It was hard to say how fresh they were, but they looked a good colour. He beat them lightly with a fork, then added some pepper and salt and put them to one side.

Rummaging around in the cupboard he found a lipped saucepan and a small basin. Pouring a little water into the saucepan, he put it on the hob to boil. The basin fitted snugly enough, the lip leaving enough of a gap for the steam to escape. It could have been made to measure. He dropped in a large knob of butter and while he waited for it to melt, added a few smaller shavings to the egg mixture.

It was at such moments that he missed Pommes Frites. He must have been very hungry to have taken the meat. It was quite out of character. Perhaps stardom was having an adverse effect on his behaviour. Either that, or some temporary aberration had caused him to think he was back working for *Le Guide*.

Opening a bottle of the Mont Caume, Monsieur Pamplemousse poured himself a glass. It looked as dark as night. Only in the south did you get quite such dark wine: a product of the late-ripening Mourvèdre vines. As the butter in the basin began to spread he tipped the egg mixture into the bowl and began stirring it with a plastic spatula.

Considering all the hazards and the things that could go wrong, it was a wonder films got made at all. Shadows, hairs in gates, passing aircraft – it wasn't until someone called for quiet that you realised just how noisy a place the world could be – doctored food; it wasn't surprising Von Strudel had gone over budget. Although you could hardly count the last episode as in any way normal.

Opening the tin of olives, he sliced several of them into small pieces. They were fat and succulent. He added them to the mixture. It was starting to thicken.

The vet had promised to examine the meat – if necessary he would get it analysed – but if Pommes Frites' rapid recovery was anything to go by, it didn't look like a serious attempt at poisoning. Another minor act of sabotage?

Monsieur Pamplemousse sat down to eat. The scrambled egg would have benefited from the addition of a little cream during its final stages and he would have given a lot for a slice or two of *baguette*, but . . . as he scraped up the remains with his fork he found himself wondering what had happened to the Director. Any guilt he might have felt about not searching him out and issuing an invitation to share the improvised lunch was quickly dispelled. The Director was more than able to look after number one. He was probably even now indulging himself in something much more exotic.

The telephone rang. It was Beaseley.

'I've found out the answer to your question.'

Monsieur Pamplemousse felt confused. He had no idea what Beaseley was on about.

'You know . . . where the idea for casting Brother Angelo came from. Apparently there was a period when he "trod the boards" for a while. Someone on the unit saw him back in the UK. He was appearing in a touring production of a musical called *Godspell*. He played Christ and by all accounts was a bit of a "wow". Slayed them in the aisles as they say, until disaster struck.'

'*Désastre?*'

'Unfortunately it happened during a matinée, so there were a lot of school parties. He was in the middle of doing some conjuring tricks when a piece of the scenery fell on his head. The air was so blue most of the children in the audience burst into tears and were whisked out by their teachers, the other half asked for their money back under the Trade Description Act. Question period the next day must have been rather fraught. It was shortly after that he was fitted with his bleeper.

'Anyway, whoever caught him in *Godspell* suggested him for the part and as soon as Von Strudel saw his photograph that was it.'

'As simple as that?'

'It's how lots of casting gets done. People play hunches. How's the invalid?'

'I think he will live.'

'Good. Tell him to keep taking the tablets.'

Monsieur Pamplemousse thanked Beaseley. He poured himself another glass of wine, then, after a moment's thought, checked in his diary and picked up the receiver again.

He dialled for an outside line, then 19 – a pause while he got International – then 44 for England. It was time he spoke to his old friend, Mr Pickering.

One of the very special things about Mr Pickering was that he was always the same. He was never taken aback.

There were no questions asked. Niceties were kept to a minimum, but were no less sincere for all that. He was also extremely knowledgeable on a surprising number of subjects.

'*Oui. Ça va, ça va.*'

'Brother Angelo? The pop star? His real name is Ron Pickles.'

Monsieur Pamplemousse couldn't help smiling. As usual Mr Pickering was turning up trumps. 'You are one of his fans?'

'Not really. It stuck in my mind because of the similarity . . . Pickering . . . Pickles.'

'*Godspell*? Good Lord! I saw that in . . . let's see . . . must have been in the fifties.'

'Really? I hadn't realised it was still running anywhere. There are so many of them now. *Joseph and the Amazing Technicolor Dreamcoat. Jesus Christ – SuperStar*. I lose track. I shall have to ask my daughter.'

'Delightful. We enjoyed it enormously. David Essex. I've got the record somewhere.'

'Yes, of course. I'll ring you back.'

Monsieur Pamplemousse washed up the debris from his cooking – there was a notice pinned to the side of the cupboard concerning maid service when required – but he had no great desire to have someone else bustling about the trailer. No doubt the same person who had tidied up and made the bed that morning came every day, bringing fresh linen and replenishing the stores. Anything else could wait.

Searching out his binoculars, Monsieur Pamplemousse wandered outside for a breath of unconditioned air. If he stayed indoors for very much longer he would find himself lying back on the bed and that would be fatal. He felt at a loose end. Normally he could have walked it off with Pommes Frites, but that, for the moment at least, was a pleasure he would have to forgo. They would have a lot of catching up to do when things returned to normal. The thought gave rise to others – a bitter-sweet mixture; a certain nobility that he had not stood in Pommes Frites' way coupled with a feeling of being slightly let down.

He scanned the surrounding countryside. The area where all the extras had gathered was almost full. It looked as though most had now arrived and taken up temporary residence. Someone – it could have been the unit manager – was addressing a group of them through a loud hailer, but he was facing the other way and it was impossible to catch the words.

Monsieur Pamplemousse trained his binoculars on the Director's car. It was now almost hidden from view behind a sea of new arrivals.

He heard a voice behind him.

'Surveying the field, Pamplemousse?'

Monsieur Pamplemousse turned. Talk of the devil! As always the Director was dressed for the occasion. White Panama hat, dark glasses, a Pierre Cardin flowered shirt worn outside immaculately pressed designer jeans . . . his gaze travelled down . . . thonged leather sandals! Light began to dawn.

The Director pretended not to have noticed the reaction.

'All is well I trust?'

'I did not expect to see you here, *Monsieur*,' said Monsieur Pamplemousse coldly.

'I happened to have some business to attend to in this part of the world, so I thought I would drop by and see how things are going.'

And land a part in the film, thought Monsieur Pamplemousse.

'They are going much as I am sure you planned them to go, *Monsieur*,' he replied.

'Good. Good. I knew I could rely on you.' The Director rubbed his hands together. 'I am reliably informed that they could have need of an extra or two to mingle with the crowd, so I may stay on for a few days.'

Monsieur Pamplemousse contemplated his chief. It occurred to him that if the Director had been born an orange he would have been a remarkably thick-skinned one. A Navel rather than a Seville.

'You plan to stay, *Monsieur*? Accommodation is impossible to get. You told me so yourself.'

The Director brushed aside the problem. 'I have had a word with the unit manager. He has allocated me a trailer. My name has already been attached to the outside door.' He looked at his watch. 'Which reminds me, I must ring Véronique.'

Monsieur Pamplemousse waved towards the camp site.

'Then it is a good thing you have a trailer, *Monsieur*. I doubt if you will be able to use your car telephone. There is already a long queue.'

'What's that?' The Director gave a start. 'What did you say?'

'You can hardly blame them. Most have probably been away from home for a long time . . . America . . . Japan . . . Pakistan. They will want to ring home. Doubtless, they will have a lot to relate.'

'*Sacré bleu!*'

'I am sure Madame Grante will understand when you explain, *Monsieur* . . . she is not as black as she is painted.'

Monsieur Pamplemousse's words fell on stony ground, as he thought they might. He wasn't normally given to playing practical jokes, but it must be catching. He had to admit to deriving a certain wry satisfaction over the speed at which the Director took off. Beaseley would appreciate it when he told him.

His own telephone was ringing when he opened the door to his trailer.

As suspected, Pommes Frites' indisposition boiled down to a matter of something he'd eaten. He could have told the vet that. What he wished to know was the precise cause of the trouble.

'Soup?' At first Monsieur Pamplemousse thought he had misheard.

'*Savon!*'

Soap! Everything had been laced with it. The lamb must have had a whole bar inside it. Slithers of soap had been inserted into the bread too. Brother Angelo was confined to his quarters. It was no wonder he had complained. There was a real Judas in the camp and no mistake. It was a sobering thought that if such a thing had happened in reality the whole course of history might have been changed.

Monsieur Pamplemousse had hardly replaced the receiver when the telephone rang again. This time it was Von Strudel.

'Zat *hund* of yours . . . Pommes Fritz . . .'

'*Oui?*' Monsieur Pamplemousse wondered what was coming.

'He is vorth his veight in gold. He is *ein* hero. Ze whole cast could have been poisoned. I am raising his salary.'

It was the first Monsieur Pamplemousse had heard talk of any kind of payment. Perhaps it really was time Pommes Frites got himself an agent. He made a mental note to get the matter in writing before Von Strudel heard the true reason for his indisposition.

'I hov decided to promote him. I am making him my personal food taster. From now on he vil taste everyzing before me.'

'Pommes Frites is a dog of many talents,' said Monsieur Pamplemousse, 'but I think you will find tasting food is his particular forte.' He nearly added the rider that if it meant tasting the output of Montgomery's kitchen, there wouldn't be much left for Von Strudel. On the other hand, if Von Strudel was dining *chez* La Baumanière that evening, the chances were they wouldn't take kindly to Pommes Frites being given first go at everything. He could foresee problems.

'Good. Zat is settled zen?'

'I am happy if Pommes Frites is happy,' said Monsieur Pamplemousse, staunchly. 'He is receiving medical attention after his last meal, so he may not be able to start work immediately, but recovery is often swift.' He hesitated. 'There is one other thing . . .'

'*Ja.*'

'I have been thinking . . . as my services as a food adviser are not keeping me fully occupied, and as the purpose of my being here is really to keep an eye on things, I wonder if it would be possible to combine the two during the shooting of the Crucifixion. It is the last time anyone will have an opportunity . . .'

Even as he spoke, Monsieur Pamplemousse realised he was laying himself open to a charge of failing miserably in his duty over the latest incident, and he was fully prepared for an explosion at the other end of the line, but to his relief he could almost feel Von Strudel beaming at the thought.

'You know somezing. You are *ein* good man. I liked you the first time I saw you. Vy? Because you stood up to me. You tell ze truth. You don't know vat it is like to be surrounded all your life by "*Ja Herrs*".'

Monsieur Pamplemousse didn't offer an answer and clearly none was expected.

'If you like I will give you *ein* part in ze film. You can vear *eine* galabiah and you can mingle mit ze crowd. Better still,' inspiration struck, 'you can be on zee route. You can be *ein* peanut seller. Zat vay no one vill suspect you. No one suspects peanut sellers.'

Ignoring the temptation to ask why, Monsieur Pamplemousse ventured to push his luck once again. 'May I have an assistant?'

'Of course. Have *zvei, drei, vier*. Take as many as you vould like. Phone ze casting director. Nothing must go vrong. I am relying on you.'

'One will be quite sufficient,' said Monsieur Pamplemousse. 'And I know just the man.'

His conscience was beginning to prick him. At the time he had made up the story about the car telephone almost without thinking. It had seemed like rough justice for the cavalier way in which the Director had plotted his being in Les Baux. Now that honour had been settled, the least he could do was make sure his chief got a part.

The last call of the day was again incoming. It was Mr Pickering.

'Sorry it's taken me so long . . . Not very good news, I'm afraid. *Godspell* hasn't been done professionally in years. It isn't even published in script form. Due for a revival.

'I can get hold of what they call a "perusal" copy if you like. You can have it on loan for a month if that's any help.'

'I don't think I shall be mounting a production,' said Monsieur Pamplemousse.

'No? Well, if you change your mind, you have only to ask. Rum business. You may be interested to know that in England the current odds against a Second Coming are a thousand to one.'

'How about the reappearance of Elvis Presley?' asked Monsieur Pamplemousse.

'The same.'

'And Ron Pickles?'

'I think the bookmakers are hedging their bets. Hope it doesn't upset your calculations . . .'

'*Oui*. Same to you.'

'Give my regards to Doucette. *Bonne chance*.'

Monsieur Pamplemousse replaced the receiver and gazed at it thoughtfully for a moment or two.

He wasn't sure if it upset any of his calculations or not. He didn't have many to upset. But if what Pickering said were true, then either Brother Angelo was a congenital liar, or he must have wanted to be in the commercial very badly indeed; badly enough to have enlisted the aid of an accomplice. It would be interesting to know exactly who in the company had suggested him for the part in the first place.

5
THE CRUCIFIXION

It was the last Friday before the start of the August holiday and there were ROUTE BARRÉE signs everywhere. Traffic in both directions on the winding D27A leading to Les Baux was at a standstill. Tempers outside the car park were frayed to breaking point. Coach drivers, their passengers pressing downcast faces against the inside of the windows, shouted at all and sundry as they tried in vain to back their vehicles. Lorry drivers, who had merely been taking a short cut, sat with folded arms. Car horns sounded. Gendarmes barked instructions. Whistles blew. Bedlam reigned supreme.

Monsieur Pamplemousse could almost feel the waves of dislike bordering on hatred as he wormed his way up the centre of the only wide section of road and, having shown his pass, was waved on his way by a poker-faced gendarme, oblivious to all but the appropriate signature on a piece of paper. He could hardly blame the other drivers. Most of them had probably come a long way hoping to arrive early and beat the crowds.

Les Baux was closed to anyone not involved in the filming. Presumably someone in authority had failed to pass on the news far enough afield. To be practical, it was hard to see how they could have done so, given the probable vagueness as to when it would actually take place, but explaining that to those who were being refused entry wasn't easy.

He drove straight through the main Porte Mage gate and on up the steep cobbled streets of the restored part of the town until eventually he managed to squeeze into an empty space in the Place St Vincent.

Normally at that time of day it would have been full of visitors, training their cameras on the sixteenth-century church with its 'lantern of the dead' bell tower and its Max Ingrand windows. Today, it was jam-packed with vehicles belonging to the unit.

Monsieur Pamplemousse continued his journey on foot up the rue du Trencat towards the *Ville Morte* – the Deserted City – where most of the activity seemed to be. He stepped round a ladder being used by a workman who was spraying grey latex over the side of a building in order to cover up an advertisement. What the shopkeepers were losing on the tourist trade they would be making up for three-fold in disturbance money. Despite that, some of them looked as though they were already beginning to regret the whole idea.

'*Oui, Madame,*' shouted the workman wearily. 'It will peel off again. You will never know it has been there.' It sounded as though he'd answered the same question many times before that morning.

Temporary dressing-rooms for the main cast had been set up in the the elegant *Mairie*. Cables disappeared through open windows. There were lights everywhere.

Further up the hill, past the ancient bread ovens, the crew were already hard at work setting up their equipment. All the stops were being pulled out to get the filming completed. The shooting of the Last Supper had gone on until late the previous evening. The sets had been struck overnight and now everything was being made ready for the Crucifixion.

Jean-Paul was supervising the setting up and positioning of the cameras. The platform of a large Louma crane with a remotely controlled camera pan and tilt mechanism rose high into the air, then swung down again as the operators watching a television monitor on the ground below made sure they didn't show anything untoward, or were themselves in danger of being revealed. Another camera, mounted on a dolly and pushed by two stalwart grips, went past on a set of rails, rehearsing a long tracking shot up the street. The focus puller sat astride the arm, checking his equipment.

Near the top they branched off to their left and continued the shot on to open ground towards the highest point where the Crucifixion itself was to take place.

Electricians were busy concealing their cables or laying ramps across them wherever there might be passing traffic.

Further on up the hill a third camera mounted on a 'cherry picker' stood by, ready to get an overall view of the scene – the streets of Jerusalem; a Jerusalem which was half the real village of Les Baux and half the product of the scenery department. It was hard to tell where one ended and the other began.

An operator with a hand-held Steadicam concealed beneath a voluminous white robe was practising taking close-up shots where those lining the streets would be standing. It struck Monsieur Pamplemousse that he wouldn't be the only one 'mingling' with the crowd that day.

Ahead of him the large perpendicular sided, unfenced plateau was packed with extras. The inevitable loud hailer boomed out barely comprehensible instructions, coupled with warnings about not straying too near the edge. The costume department, having set up headquarters beside the ruins of an old windmill, were having their work cut out exchanging T-shirts for more seemly wear. Near the monument to the Provençal poet, Charloun Rieu, make-up were equally busy, adding a beard here, a moustache there. A team of girls was working overtime with jars of skin toning; others were hard at work dressing hair. They all looked tired. There was no sign of Anne-Marie. She must be busy with the principals down at the Town Hall.

In a far corner of the plateau an assistant director was rehearsing a group in the art of murmuring. It grew more bloodthirsty by the minute. From a distance it sounded like a football crowd baying for blood.

The dolly came back down the hill, then a moment later reappeared again on its way up for yet another dry run. This time the arm was facing the other way so that the camera could shoot back on itself, following the progress of Jesus carrying the cross.

'*Lentement . . . Lentement . . .*' The cameraman waved his hand, palm downwards. The men pushing him were only too pleased to obey. They looked worn-out already.

Jean-Paul surveyed the scene pensively through a view-finder, checking his findings from time to time with a light meter. The ambient colour in Les Baux changed by the hour according to the position of the sun. Sometimes yellow, often blindingly white; in the evening the stone could take on an almost fiery-red hue. It would need careful exposure. There was a limit to what the laboratories could do when it came to matching shots taken at different times of the day.

Monsieur Pamplemousse spotted the Director in an area to his left, between the end of the restored section of the town and the ruins of the old. Dressed as a Roman senator, he was standing gloomily beside a canopied barrow laden with nuts.

His costume, an embroidered silk tunic beneath a voluminous rectangular cloak, looked as though it had been hired from a Paris theatrical agency. So much for his story of 'happening' to find himself in the area. It was hardly the garb of an itinerant peanut seller. Clearly he'd had his sights set on higher things.

Hoping he hadn't been seen, Monsieur Pamplemousse took advantage of a passing donkey laden with bread-filled panniers. As it ambled slowly by, momentarily acting as a screen, he made for the plateau.

It was worse than sale time at Galeries Lafayette. There were queues everywhere.

He recognised the continuity girl. She had been at the screening of the rushes. She was joined by the script girl and the call boy, both carrying a clipboard. They waved as they caught sight of him. All three looked harassed.

The call boy reappeared a moment later and took Monsieur Pamplemousse to the front of the costume queue. It was nice having friends in high places. He chose a simple white, high-necked robe and some sandals. There was no sense in trying to compete with the Director. Placing his surplus belongings into a sealed bag, he joined another queue to check them in with Security.

On his way back he bumped into Beaseley. He, too, looked harassed. His cravat had a distinctly ruffled look to it.

'*Comment ça va?*'

'Script changes,' said Beaseley. 'They're leaving the actual Crucifixion until tomorrow. The way things are going they'll be lucky to get the journey to Golgotha and the burial in the can.

'Rumours abound. The good news is that Mangetout has locked herself in her trailer and won't come out. On the other side of the coin, Brother Angelo is complaining of a bad back and says he can't carry the cross all that way. Von Strudel is with him now. Voices were being raised even as I came past the *Mairie*. My money, as always, is on Von Strudel. He has the megaphone.'

'As I recall,' said Monsieur Pamplemousse, 'Jesus had a similar problem. They called on Simon, from Cyrene, to carry it for him.'

'Good point,' said Beaseley. 'Yet another paradox. Do you realise today is a Friday. It was on a Friday – 3 April

AD 33 according to the latest scientific evidence – that Christ is supposed to have died. That was why there was such a rush to bury him. The Sabbath started at nightfall . . .' He broke off and took a closer look at Monsieur Pamplemousse. 'So this what the average food adviser wore in Roman times? I've often wondered.'

It occurred to Monsieur Pamplemousse that he had never let on to Beaseley the true purpose of his being there. It didn't seem an ideal moment to come clean, even if he'd wished to. He still wasn't sure how far to trust his companion. 'It was a lowly position,' he said. 'The Romans were seldom in need of advice, least of all on food.'

'True,' said Beaseley. 'True. Fortunately for you, they bequeathed France their recipes. They only left us their roads. Which is why if it moves you French eat it, whereas we British lay bets on it. Care for a drink?'

He gestured towards yet another queue, longer than the rest, lining up outside one of the catering wagons.

Monsieur Pamplemousse made his excuses. 'There is someone I have to see.'

He found the Director lolling disconsolately on a shooting stick partially concealed beneath his robes. There was a small pile of peanut shells at his feet.

'Trade is far from brisk, Aristide,' he said gloomily. 'A difficult role to sustain when custom is thin on the ground. I hope things will pick up when shooting begins.'

Monsieur Pamplemousse couldn't resist a sly dig. 'It could be that you are looking too prosperous, *Monsieur*. Customers may find you intimidating.'

It was like water off a duck's back. The Director gazed at him. 'At least I have made the effort, Pamplemousse,' he said severely. 'I hardly think your present attire would have labelled you a trendsetter in AD 30. Heads would not have turned when you passed by.'

'It is a good "mingling" colour, *Monsieur*,' said Monsieur Pamplemousse stiffly.

94

The Director had the grace to acknowledge the point. Having taken a quick look over his shoulder, he lowered his voice. 'I cannot begin to tell you what a comfort it is to know you are keeping an eye on things, Aristide. It will not go unremarked in certain circles I can assure you.'

'That is nice to know, *Monsieur*,' said Monsieur Pamplemousse drily.

'Do you have any news?' asked the Director.

Monsieur Pamplemousse shook his head.

'No thoughts as to where the miscreant may strike next?'

'It depends,' said Monsieur Pamplemousse, thoughtfully, 'as to which miscreant you are referring. I suspect there may be more than one.'

It was the first time the Director had made positive mention of the true reason behind his assignment, and he was wondering whether or not to tackle him on the subject, when there was a shifting of attention as those gathered on the plateau began a concerted movement in their direction.

'Well, let us hope the wrong one doesn't get the upper hand,' said the Director, helping himself to another peanut.

Von Strudel strode into view, fixing the approaching masses with a gimlet eye. Clearly he must have won his battle with Brother Angelo. Raising the megaphone to his lips he began bellowing orders. Cries of '*Dummkopf!*' filled the air. People began to put on speed.

'It is an interesting fact,' said the Director, 'that even in this age of protest and rebellion, one man can inspire absolute terror and obedience amongst so many. Film making is one of the last havens of the true despot. Hitler would have been good at it.'

If Monsieur Pamplemousse detected a note of envy, he didn't dwell on the fact. His heart sank as he took stock of the crowd. The Director was right to be worried. If anyone did intend causing a disruption, now was their big chance, and there would be no possibility whatsoever of stopping them. He only hoped nothing happened to cause a panic. The prospect of people falling and being trampled on by a crowd rushing headlong down the narrow streets towards the only means of exit from Les Beaux or, worse still, disappearing lemming-like over the edge of the surrounding cliffs, didn't bear thinking about.

It was late morning by the time the extras had been herded into place and received their final instructions . . . 'You are not here to enjoy yourselves. You are here to vork. I do not vish to see anyvun *mit* ze smile on zer face. Anyone found smilingk will be given ze order *mit* ze bootz.'

The possibility of anyone enjoying themselves seemed remote, but Von Strudel was taking no chances.

A hush fell over the assembly as shooting began; a hush which communicated itself to all those lining the route.

As the cameras drew near, the Director edged away from the barrow and assumed a more imposing stance. Clearly, he didn't wish to be identified in such a lowly role.

Monsieur Pamplemousse watched carefully as the mob moved slowly past. It was hard to tell how much of Brother Angelo's performance was acting and how much was in earnest. His face was certainly white from the strain. The stage blood on his back had started to congeal from the heat of the sun, which was now directly overhead. The crown of thorns looked all too real. The sweat running down his face undoubtedly was. The two thieves following on behind looked equally haggard.

Despite everything, it was surprisingly moving. The noise of the crowd, the heat, the flies, the sheer intensity of it all, combined with the concentration of the crew made the scene seem strangely real. It was like witnessing a live event, having grown blasé over the years through seeing the same thing on television too many times in the comfort of one's own home. The extras left behind as the pageant moved on up the hill looked equally affected as they drifted slowly away. Many remained where they were to watch, unable to tear themselves away.

Stopping for one reason or another, starting, repositioning, a much needed tea break . . . the day melted away, and it was evening before a temporary halt in the shooting was called. Apart from taking a few 'wild shots' of Brother Angelo for editing purposes, it was time to move on.

That there had been no accidents was a minor miracle in itself. As an exercise in crowd control it had been beyond reproach.

Leaving the Director to carry on by himself, Monsieur Pamplemousse made his way towards the ruins of the old city, where preparations had been made to shoot the burial sequence.

Beaseley was already there, along with Von Strudel and Jean-Paul. The crowd, having been put on stand-by until the next day, had largely dispersed.

There was a sense of urgency among those gathered round the cave. The sun would shortly disappear over the horizon. Timing was as critical for the unit as it must have been for the friends of Jesus who needed to carry out the ceremony before the Sabbath began.

There was still enough natural light to see shadowy details, but Jean-Paul added a little more. The level was changing with every passing moment. Standing alongside Monsieur Pamplemousse, he called for the camera to be lowered still more until it was shooting up.

'Do you know the painting by Caravaggio? That is the effect I am trying to achieve,' Jean-Paul whispered.

Watched by Mary, Mother of Joseph, and Mary of Magdala, Joseph and Nicodemus were rehearsing the rolling of a vast rock across the mouth of a tomb supposedly carved in the side of a hill outside Jerusalem where the body of Jesus was to be laid to rest. It was easy to see now why Les Baux had been chosen. It was a natural setting. The rock was circular, it could have been the grindstone from an old flour mill. Getting it moving at all was one thing. Stopping it in exactly the right spot so that it blocked the opening to the cave was something else again.

'Faster,' bellowed Von Strudel. 'Faster. *Mein Gott!* You are like ze snails. It is Friday eveningk. *Samstag* vil have come und gone by ze time you hov finished. You need to be faster. Faster, but *mit* ze reverence.'

'The sound of popping blood vessels,' murmured Beaseley, 'is really quite unique.'

'Places everyone.'

Jean-Paul made a quick check of the exposure, called for the gaffer to remove a layer of scrim from a lamp to bring up the light a bit more and restore the balance, then gave the thumbs-up sign.

'This is a take. Let's make it a good one.'

The clapper boy rushed on.

'Cue action.'

Joseph and Nicodemus entered shot carrying the body of Jesus, wrapped now in linen cloths to cover the wounds left by the soldiers. A strong smell of burial spices – a mixture of myrrh and aloes – mingled with that of human sweat. Placing the body reverently on a slab just inside the cave, they quickly withdrew and took hold of the rock. Their bodies glistened as it threatened to roll past its mark and they took up the strain.

'Cut!'

Everyone waited patiently while Von Strudel, Jean-Paul, the second director and others went into a huddle. Monsieur Pamplemousse looked around. It was as though time had stopped. Everyone had frozen in their position. In the short length of time it had taken to run the scene the sun had already set. The surrounding ruins, pock-marked and shadowy, had taken on the appearance of a gaunt and eyeless audience.

'OK. Print it.'

'Thank you, everyone.'

'*Ja.* Zat vas good.'

An almost audible sigh of relief went up all round the set as everyone relaxed and began talking at once.

Jean-Paul turned to his crew. '*Merci. Terminez . . . Emballer . . .* Wrap it up.'

The words were hardly out of his mouth when the lights all round the entrance to the cave suddenly went out. For a moment or two there was chaos. Voices came out of the darkness. '*Merde! Sacré bleu! Scheibe!* What the . . .'

Just as suddenly they came on again. Jean-Paul hurried back on to the set. 'Some *imbécile* must have tripped over a breaker switch. The plug had been pulled out.'

'Thank Christ it wasn't during the take.' The Assistant Director's shake of the wrist echoed everyone's feelings. 'OK. Strike the rock.'

A prop man ambled on and trundled the stone away with one hand. It bounced on some pebbles, then rolled over on to its side, jogging up and down as it settled. He raised a laugh by adopting a 'muscle-man' stance.

'What would we do without polystyrene?' said Beaseley.

'You don't think . . .'

'What?'

'*Je n'en sais pas.*' Monsieur Pamplemousse suddenly felt uneasy, that was all. He had no idea why.

'All films are an illusion,' said Beaseley. 'The quickness of the shot deceives the eye. Half the time the screen is blank anyway. If man hadn't been born with persistency of vision someone would have had to invent it . . .'

Beaseley's theme remained undeveloped as their attention was suddenly distracted by an outbreak of chatter from the mouth of the cave.

'*C'est impossible!*'

'Hey, everyone, come and look at this!'

'Jesus!'

'*Mein Gott!*' Von Strudel pushed his way to the front of

the group and stared into the darkness. For once he seemed at a loss for words.

'I think,' said Beaseley, as he and Monsieur Pample-mousse joined the others and craned their necks to see what was going on, 'that what we have is a classic case of the "Old Mother Hubbards".'

'*Comment*?'

'Old Mother Hubbard,' said Beaseley, 'went to the cupboard, to fetch her poor dog a bone. But when she got there, the cupboard was bare, and so the poor dog had none. For bone, read Brother Angelo. In short, we are witnessing yet another attack of the dreaded *bugginks*!'

6
THE SACRIFICE

It hadn't taken Monsieur Pamplemousse long to find what he was looking for: a gelatin filter lying on the ground near the Ark. It was slightly blackened in the middle from the heat of a lamp – which was probably why it had been discarded – the dark patch would change the colour temperature of the light – but it was ideally suited to his purpose: tough yet pliable.

It took him even less time to put it to good use. Crouching down, he bent one edge of the plastic slightly, then slipped it behind the stop batten of the door frame and round between the casing and the leading edge of the door itself, applying pressure at the same time so that it slid even further between the two. Luckily, as with most modern exterior doors, slight warping had taken place, leaving a larger gap near the bottom than there was halfway up. The lock was a standard cylinder rim type, identical to the one on his own trailer. Nothing special. There was no deadlock bolt – neither the automatic variety nor the kind which was operated by a second turn of the key. It was an open invitation to anyone with an old credit card – or a discarded gelatin filter found on a film location.

He slid the plastic up the gap, once again applying pressure. The higher he went the more resistance he encountered. The first time it jammed just below the lock. He changed the angle slightly and tried again with one swift, sweeping motion. This time it slid between the rounded bolt and the staple. There was a satisfactory click as the mechanism responded. The bolt slid back into the body of the lock and the door swung open.

Probably at that very moment there were other equally satisfactory clicks taking place all over the world. He knew from his time in the *Sûreté* that Friday night in Paris was always a particularly busy night for the police, with people going off for the week-end and leaving their apartments unattended. Except it wasn't Paris, and he would have been as hard put to justify what he was doing as any common or garden *cambrioleur*.

Monsieur Pamplemousse took a quick look over his shoulder to make sure no one else was around. The next moment he was inside Brother Angelo's trailer, closing the door gently behind him.

Only after he had made absolutely certain that the curtains were tightly drawn did he turn on his torch. His Cupillard Rième watch showed 1.18.

The trailer was basically identical to his own, if considerably less tidy. There were discarded magazines strewn everywhere. Unwashed glasses stood where they had been left. The remains of long since melted ice-cubes gave off an odour of whisky. There was also a smell of stale cigar smoke, Cigar smoke and . . . Monsieur Pamplemousse sniffed . . . powder rather than perfume.

He made his way through the kitchen to the back end of the trailer. The make-up area had certainly been put to good use. The table was littered with discarded tissues. The waste bucket was chock-a-block. Whoever had the task of clearing up in the morning was in for a busy time. He checked the bath and the washbasin. Neither appeared to have used recently. The towels felt dry.

He slid open the cupboard doors. It was hard to say if any clothes were missing. The hanging wardrobe was reasonably full, as were the drawers below it; socks, underclothes, monogrammed handkerchiefs . . . all the things one might expect. Perhaps they weren't as full as they might have been, but they were nowhere near empty either. There were certainly no telltale signs of a hasty packing. There was nothing hidden behind the hanging clothes, nothing in any of the pockets, nothing untoward tucked away in any of the drawers.

He drew a blank in the kitchen area. Apart from a few vegetables in the bottom drawer, the refrigerator was empty. The end of a *baguette* lay dry and abandoned on the working area. Alongside it was an open tin containing a few black olives. They were from the ubiquitous Monsieur Arnaud.

There was some unwashed crockery in the sink. Two of everything.

Hoping it might prove more productive than the rest of the trailer, Monsieur Pamplemousse went back into the main area and began an inch by inch search of the room.

In a sense he was hampered by not having the remotest idea what he hoped to find. It was easier to say what he wasn't looking for.

If Ron Pickles's disappearance had been planned, it was doubtful if he would have left any evidence of that fact behind. Everything he had seen so far bore all the hallmarks of someone who had nothing to conceal. That being so, there was no point in looking for conventional hiding-places – inside hollow brass curtain rods, objects taped to the underside of drawers or wrapped in aluminium foil and put inside the freezer compartment of the refrigerator.

Also, space being at a premium, a trailer lacked many of the possibilities of an ordinary house – the glass fibre insulation between the roof rafters, for example, made a good hiding place; or fake plumbing – a false plastic waste pipe could hold a surprising amount. Luxurious the trailer might be, but everything about it was starkly functional. It had to perform a useful task, or else . . .

103

Hollowed-out books? The only book he could see was, rather surprisingly, an English edition of Daudet's *Letters from a Windmill*, a slim volume, one page of which was marked by a ticket stub from a show called the *Cathédrale d'Images* which was taking place in one of the local disused bauxite mines. *Prix d'Entrée* 33F *Adulte*. Neither the book nor the *Cathédrale d'Images* sounded exactly Ron Pickles's cup of tea. There was really no predicting other people's tastes.

He came across a second book on the floor beside the bed, a guide to the area, again in English. A section devoted to the Massif de la Sainte-Baume, west of Marseille, was marked by a tourist's brochure describing the delights of Fontvieille. There was a picture of Daudet's windmill on the front. It must have been picked up in Fontvieille itself because it bore the stamp of the Office de Tourisme. Perhaps Daudet's letters had made an effect on Brother Angelo?

A waste-bucket in a corner of the room yielded up a half-used packet of book matches bearing the name of a restaurant called La Croissant d'Or in the coastal town of Les Saintes-Maries-de-la-Mer, some screwed-up pages of script on yellow paper, and three more ticket stubs for the *Cathédrale d'Images*. Monsieur Pamplemousse wondered who Brother Angelo's companions had been. Mangetout, along with the Swedish *au pair* and the child? Except all the tickets were marked *Adulte*.

Monsieur Pamplemousse shone the torch on to his watch again. The search had taken over half an hour. There wasn't a lot to show for it.

He lay back on the bed turning the problem over in his mind, trying to picture what, if anything, his search had yielded. He looked in vain for a common link between a windmill, a meal by the sea, a walk in the mountains and a visit to a show. They were all ordinary enough: the kind of outings anyone might make if they were staying in the area and had time to spare.

And yet . . . and yet somehow that didn't ring true. None of the parties involved was exactly ordinary. None could have had that much time to spare. Mangetout kept herself so much to herself she made the late Marlene Dietrich look like Zsa Zsa Gabor, and from all he'd seen of Brother Angelo, he didn't exactly court being seen in public. He must dread going out at times. Worse than being royalty. At least they weren't besieged by autograph hunters.

Monsieur Pamplemousse switched off the torch and closed his eyes. The window must be open a fraction, for above the hum of the air-conditioning and the faint sound of the generator he could hear music in the distance – a guitar and a girl singing – coming from the camp site where all the fans were living.

He wasn't sure how long he had been lying there . . . fifteen minutes? . . . twenty? . . . when he heard a noise. It was the faint, but unmistakable rasping sound made by a key being pushed very gently through the pin tumblers of a door lock.

Mentally cursing himself for not throwing the bolt after he had entered, Monsieur Pamplemousse lay where he was, his right hand grasping the edge of the bed, ready to spring up at a second's notice. With his other hand he searched for the torch.

There was a shaft of moonlight, momentarily obscured by a shadowy figure, then the key was quickly withdrawn and the door closed again. Fully expecting the room to be flooded with light, Monsieur Pamplemousse braced himself. But instead, the newcomer moved swiftly across the room and leant across the bed as though searching for something. He felt the other person's warmth and there was a smell similar to the one he had noticed earlier, only much stronger this time. Resisting the temptation to reach up, he held his breath. There was a sudden gasp as whoever it was realised they were not alone.

'*Tu!*' The cry was one of pleasurable surprise rather than fear.

The figure straightened.

'*Mon chou! Mon chou!*'

Something heavy was discarded.

'*Mon chou!*' There was a wriggle as something lighter went the same way. A moment later he felt a body pressing itself against him: warm, sensuous, alive. Inviting lips sought his. Hands reached out and down . . .

The moment ended even faster than it had begun. The gasp this time was of total horror. The figure leapt from the bed and made a wild dash for safety. The door shot open and slammed shut again.

Monsieur Pamplemousse struggled to his feet. There was a thump as something heavy landed on the floor. Groping around, he made contact with his torch and switched it on.

A crumpled silk *négligé* lay in a heap where it had been abandoned. Beneath it was a top coat of some kind. He bent down. The *négligé* bore a La Perla label. Hardly what one might have expected anyone from the camp site to be wearing. On the other hand, he would have been willing to swear on oath that his visitor hadn't been Mangetout. It had been someone a good deal younger. He picked up the coat and was about to discard it when something prompted him to feel in the side pockets.

The first one contained a key, the second a ticket stub. It was yet another for the *Cathédrale d'Images*. There was a number across the top – 067174. He compared it with the numbers on those he had already found. One of them was 067175. It was only then that he realised that none of the other three numbers were consecutive. Brother Angelo must have been by himself when he went there on the other occasions.

Taking one last look round the room, Monsieur Pamplemousse let himself out. There was no point in lingering.

Closing the door gently behind him, he stood for a moment or two pressed hard against the side of the trailer, merging with the shadows, but nothing moved.

The night air was heavy with the smell of lavender and herbs. Cicadas were in full throat. Les Baux, starkly white and pockmarked by day, looked impossibly romantic in the moonlight; the twinkling lights gave it the appearance of some huge ocean liner sailing into the night. Romantic and at the same time still charged with horrors of the past. Its jagged outline against the night sky was like an illustration from a fairy tale by the brothers Grimm; a reminder that it was from the top of those very same rocks that Raymond de Turenne had rounded off his evenings by forcing prisoners to leap to their death. Their screams must have echoed round the Val d'Enfer, drowning the drunken laughter.

The heat was oppressive. In the distance, beyond the perimeter of the lot, he could see lights coming from the area where the extras were camping out, and there was the occasional flicker of a camp fire. Many of the fans had already left, but there was still a large body of those eager to see things out to the bitter end. The music sounded louder now and the mood had changed; it was somehow more restless, like the voice of a tormented being.

Detecting a glimmer of light in Mangetout's trailer, Monsieur Pamplemousse moved away in the opposite direction, making a detour round the back of the other vehicles. He thought he heard a baby crying somewhere. It stopped as quickly as it had begun. It could have been the plaintive cry of a sheep.

As he rounded the far corner of Gilbert Beaseley's quarters he almost collided with someone coming the other way.

It was the Director. A Director, moreover, who was clutching his right eye as though in pain.

'Ah, there you are, Pamplemousse. I have been looking for you everywhere.'

107

'Is there something wrong, *Monsieur*?'

'Wrong?' repeated the Director. 'Wrong? I have been attacked!'

'Attacked?' As was so often the case with his chief, Monsieur Pamplemousse found himself reduced to echoing the other's words.

'Attacked,' repeated the Director. 'I must admit, when I found a certain person occupying your quarters I thought the worst, but in no way did it prepare me for what transpired.'

Monsieur Pamplemousse stared at him. 'There is someone in my trailer, *Monsieur*?

It was the Director's turn to gaze in disbelief. 'You are not trying to plead innocent, Pamplemousse?'

'I give you my word, *Monsieur*.'

'Come, come, Aristide, you know me better than that. In matters of love and war, everything is fair. The best man has won. Let us say no more about it.'

'I repeat, *Monsieur*, I have no idea what you are talking about.'

Monsieur Pamplemousse might just as well have saved his breath. The Director had clearly got the bit between his teeth and did not intend letting go until he'd had his say.

'Unable to sleep for whatever reason – I think possibly it was the noise of the music – if that is the word to describe what sounds more like the cacophonous ramblings of those on whom the full moon has had an adverse effect – I got dressed and went for a walk. I found myself irresistibly drawn towards Les Alpilles and I went further than I had originally intended.

'When I returned, I have to admit that in approaching the site from a different direction I found myself totally disoriented. Seeing a chink of light coming from your quarters, I thought I would call in for a chat. I knocked on your door several times, but to no avail, and I was about to go on my way when to my surprise it was opened by none other than Mangetout. I was so taken aback it took me a moment or two to recognise her.

'The light, Pamplemousse, was the only thing she had on.

'It was a case of having to think on my feet. I pretended I had come to ask for her autograph. It was the best I could do on the spur of the moment. Clearly she did not have a *plume* about her person, and I was in the act of looking for mine when she attacked me. I cannot begin to tell you the language she used. I was lucky to make good my escape.'

Monsieur Pamplemousse stared at the Director. 'Mangetout was in my trailer?' he repeated. 'But that is not possible.'

'Pamplemousse,' the Director put a hand to his face again, 'there is no need to pretend. I know she is there. I saw her with my own eyes – as large as life and twice as powerful. I fully understand why you feel the need to be on your own for a while. Doubtless your batteries need recharging. Have no fear, the matter shall remain a secret between us. *C'est la vie*. I hope I am man enough to accept defeat gracefully.'

'But, *Monsieur*, there must be some mistake . . .' Monsieur Pamplemousse suddenly felt at a loss for words. 'If you come with me I will prove to you . . .'

'Not for all the *café* in Maroc, Pamplemousse. It was an illusion destroyed. One should not get too close to one's dreams. The reality seldom lives up to them. I will leave you to your own devices, such as they are. I see now why you and Pommes Frites are occupying separate trailers.' He reached out a hand. 'If I may, I will borrow your *torche de poche* and find my own way back.'

The Director broke off and stared at the object in Monsieur Pamplemousse's other hand. 'What is that you are holding, Pamplemousse?'

'It is nothing . . .' Monsieur Pamplemousse hastily stuffed the *négligé* under his jacket.

'Nothing?' exclaimed the Director. 'It is no wonder Mangetout was in a state of *déshabillée*.'

'*Monsieur!* . . . This does *not* belong to Mangetout. It is . . .'

'Well, Pamplemousse?' The Director assumed his magisterial tones.

'It belongs to someone else,' said Monsieur Pamplemousse lamely.

The Director gazed at him as if he could hardly believe his eyes.

'Is there no end to your depravity, Pamplemousse?' he boomed. 'Are you totally insatiable? Can you not be alone for five minutes? That poor woman. Small wonder she was distraught and smelling of gin.'

'It is a long story, *Monsieur* . . .'

'And I do not wish to hear it,' said the Director.

'*Monsieur* . . .'

'The *lumière*, Pamplemousse.'

Monsieur Pamplemousse took a firm grip of his torch. 'I hardly think that will be necessary, *Monsieur*.' He turned and pointed towards the nearest trailer. 'Your quarters are there in front of you.'

Relenting long enough to shine the light as far as the steps, Monsieur Pamplemousse waited until the Director was safely inside, then he turned and made straight for his own trailer, feeling for his key as he went.

Fully prepared for the worst, he flung open the door. The living-room was empty, the bed untouched. He went through into the kitchen. That, too, was exactly as he had left it. He drew a blank in the make-up area.

Returning to the main room, Monsieur Pamplemousse sat on the edge of his bed for a moment or two. It was a puzzle and no mistake. The Director could hardly have imagined all that he had described. Nor would he have made it up. His black eye was real enough. And if Mangetout had been in the trailer she would hardly have had time to vacate it. Unless, of course, the Director had

110

been wandering around in a daze for longer than he realised. It was possible.

As he began to undress, Monsieur Pamplemousse looked at his watch again. Less than half an hour had passed since he had last checked the time; it felt much longer.

He lay back on the bed and closed his eyes. The mysterious visitor to Brother Angelo's trailer had been another strange business. At the time it had seemed all too real . . . his mind drifted back to Mangetout. He wondered where she was now? Back in her own trailer? And what was she feeling about Ron's disappearance? Did she even know about it? It was quite within the bounds of possibility that she didn't. If they were in the middle of one of their periodic rows she could well have gone into a sulk. Not many people would be brave enough to knock on her door to break the news.

His head was throbbing from the incessant drumming coming from the camp site. It was getting louder; ever more urgent, but he was too tired to let it worry him. Pulling the duvet over his head, Monsieur Pamplemousse fell fast asleep in a matter of moments.

He had no idea how long it lasted; it could have been minutes, it could have been hours. All he was conscious of was being woken abruptly some time later by the sound of the telephone ringing. He struggled into a sitting position and reached for the receiver.

'Pamplemousse, are you all right?' It was the Director. He sounded agitated.

'*Oui, Monsieur.*' Monsieur Pamplemousse manfully resisted the temptation to say he would have felt better still had he not been woken.

'You have not been experiencing tremors?'

'Tremors, *Monsieur*?'

'The ground keeps shaking. This is not an area subject to earthquakes is it?'

'Not so far as I am aware, *Monsieur.*'

111

'There seems to be a wind getting up. Listen . . . can you hear it? Could it be the Mistral? I . . . Pamplemousse . . .' The Director's voice rose an octave or two. 'The whole room is moving. I . . . *Sacré bleu*! Come quickly! *Mon Dieu*! . . .'

There was a click and the line went dead.

As it did so, Monsieur Pamplemousse became aware that the noise which he had at first taken to be some kind of interference on the line, a fault in the air-conditioning perhaps, or, indeed, as the Director had suggested, the Mistral making an unseasonable sortie down the Rhône Valley, was actually much closer to hand.

Making a dive for the window, he operated the blind and was just in time to see the upper half of a trailer go past. Swaying as it went, like a ship at sea or some giant artificial monster in a Chinese New Year festivity, it was borne on a vast, undulating, heaving, tidal wave of bodies; some clad in galabiahs left over from the previous day's shoot, others wearing T-shirts bearing motifs and illustrations which even from a distance were clearly of a sexual nature. Others again had discarded everything completely. Brother Angelo's fan club were on the rampage and it was an awesome sight.

As the trailer disappeared behind some rocks Monsieur Pamplemousse caught his breath. The blind on one of the windows was raised and he had a momentary glimpse of a white face pressed against the inside of the glass. There was no need to look for his Leitz Trinovids in order to identify the owner of the countenance. It belonged to the Director, and terror was writ large all over it.

Monsieur Pamplemousse made a dive for the telephone again and dialled the duty security officer. A girl answered.

'Which service do you require, *Monsieur*?'

'I think,' said Monsieur Pamplemousse urgently, 'you had better send one of everything . . . *tout de suite*!'

7
IMAGES GALORE

Following a sign marked *Cathédrale d'Images*, Monsieur Pamplemousse took the back road out of Les Baux towards Arles. He had been driving for less than a minute when he rounded a bend and there on his right he saw a great rectangular hole carved out of the hillside. It was much grander than he had expected – cathedral was an apt description. Great slabs of white limestone left over from the days when it was a working quarry were stacked on either side of the opening. He drove into an empty car park and crunched his way across the gravel towards a small ticket office to the left of what must once have been the loading area.

He still wasn't quite sure why he was there, other than playing a hunch. A process of elimination really. It was also a means of passing the time. The Director had been admitted to a *hospice* in Arles and was under heavy sedation, so there was no point in trying to visit him. Work on the film had ground to a halt.

He scanned a notice board displaying various facts and figures about the mine. Forty slide projectors programmed to display some 2,500 slides, each one enlarged up to 10,000 times on to 4,000 square metres of surface area spread over 300 metres of walkway. A magical and unforgettable world, according to the blurb, born from the talent and imagination of its creator, the late Albert

Plecy. The *Image totale* process made it possible for the spectator to wander at will through a gigantic audio-visual show. The whole sight and sound spectacular lasted thirty minutes.

The girl in the cash desk seemed surprised to see him. It was hard to say whether she was pleased or not. Probably not from the way she put down her magazine. He decided to ply her with a few tentative questions.

'*Oui*, business had suffered since the film company had taken over Les Baux. Not many people knew the *Cathédrale* existed and there was not much through traffic on the D27. They relied on tapping the overspill of visitors to the old town who came across their advertisements. Normally on a Saturday at this time of the year there would be crowds, but now . . . poof! See for yourself! was the general tenor of her responses. Her final question, 'You are from the company?' was slightly more animated.

'I am . . . attached . . .' Monsieur Pamplemousse tried to make his connection sound as tenuous as possible.

'I would be better off as an extra.' He wasn't sure if it was a statement, a moment of dreaming, or a hint. Perhaps she was hoping he was a casting director.

Hearing some pop music coming from a portable radio in the background, he tried another tack. 'You are a fan of Brother Angelo?'

The girl brightened. '*Oui*. And he is a fan of the *Cathédrale*. He has been here several times.'

'It is possible to see the same show more than once?'

'Of course! People come back all the time.'

Realising he had made a tactical error, Monsieur Pamplemousse tried to bring the conversation back again.

'When was the last time he was here?'

'The day before he disappeared. He didn't stay for long, but then he never did.' She brushed the hair away from her eyes. 'It is a strange business. Disappearing like that.'

'You know about it?' He felt in his trouser pocket for some change.

'Who doesn't? Nobody talks about anything else around here.'

'And you have not seen him since?'

'I wouldn't be sitting here if I had, would I?'

There was no one like the young, thought Monsieur Pamplemousse, for expressing with a single glance total and utter contempt for asking ridiculous questions.

He suddenly felt his age.

'At least you will have the cave more or less to yourself,' said the girl. 'There is only one other customer this morning.

'It doesn't matter if the show has already started. You can stay in there as long as you like. One show ends – another begins.'

Monsieur Pamplemousse thanked her and then pushed his way through the turnstile. He stood for a moment or two in the open area between the box office and the entrance to the cave, taking in the unexpected grandeur of the scene. It all seemed so much larger than life; it was like coming across a film set for some Cecil B. de Mille biblical extravaganza, or a theatre modelled after an Egyptian temple which had somehow been left over from the great days of Hollywood. It would certainly make a wonderful hide-out.

Could anyone get in and out without paying? There was a long metal barrier between the ticket office and the opposite side of the area where the entrance to the old mine lay. But if the girl were distracted, or if she left her post for a moment? She would hardly leave it unattended if there were any potential customers around. It certainly wasn't something to bank on. Even if he had changed his appearance, Brother Angelo had clearly already made his mark and he wouldn't risk being recognised.

Wandering towards the back and into a cavernous hollowed-out part of the hill, he passed the window of a little room where a plain deal table was laid with two plates. There was a *baguette*, some cheese and a bottle of red wine. A man was busying himself at a stove. Early *déjeuner* for himself and the girl at the cash desk? It looked like some kind of off-duty rest room. The window commanded a view of the car park and the approach road. He couldn't see anyone else around, although there were some official-looking offices to his left. They looked as though they were closed for the day.

He walked on a little, then came to an abrupt halt. Various *Danger* and *Passage Interdit* notices barred further progress. Presumably they were meant to be off-putting, because beyond them he could see patches of blue sky, so presumably anyone approaching from the other side – over the top of the hill – could gain access that way. If no one was watching.

A moment later the question was partly answered for him. A car drew up outside the car park and the driver – presumably a tourist or someone from a nearby camp site – tried to deposit a cardboard box full of rubbish alongside a litter bin. The man he'd seen a moment before rushed out of the rest room waving his arms and shouting.

It was a private litter bin. It belonged to the Company. How dare he!

The driver disappeared into his car like a scalded cat and drove off hell for leather down the hill. It looked as though it wasn't the first time such a thing had happened.

All the same, if the man was able to spot it from a distance of some fifty or sixty metres, he would surely have seen someone trying to get in without paying. There was no means of telling without testing the system.

On the other hand, if there were two people. One to divert attention . . .

It was time he went in. If he lingered much longer he would become an object of suspicion himself.

The door into the *Cathédrale* proper was reached via a long hallway hollowed out of the cliff. It was lined with display cabinets and posters giving more facts and figures, mostly about Albert Plecy and how he had established a research centre in the quarries. There were lists of past shows – amongst them one devoted to the paintings of Vincent Van Gogh. This year it was 'The Magic of Stained Glass'. The best things in life had always just been or were 'coming shortly'.

Entering through a door at the far end Monsieur Pamplemousse suddenly found himself in almost total darkness. Darkness with a chilly edge to it. He wished he had brought something warmer to wear. Ahead of him he could hear music and there was a faint glow of light. As his eyes grew accustomed to the lack of light he began to edge his way forward. Suddenly there was a burst of music directly overhead and on a wall to his left a picture of an illuminated church window appeared. It was followed by others to his right. The music grew louder, then faded as a commentator's voice took over. The whole cave seemed alive with shapes and sound. Nothing he had read outside had quite prepared him for the experience. The smooth white walls made perfect screens, and the texture and shape provided exactly the right amount of reverberation. He was surrounded by sound and by constantly changing pictures. It was quadrophonic, three-dimensional theatre in the round, and a totally unique experience.

Monsieur Pamplemousse began to work his way deeper into the mine, past supporting pillars and on into other vast chambers. There was constant clicking from all directions as the computerised projectors changed slides, mixing automatically from one to another. He was so absorbed by the sheer complexity of it all that for a while it commanded his whole attention. It wasn't until he found an optimum point which offered an almost 360 degree view of the cave that he paused for a moment, and leaning against a pillar, away from the criss-crossing beams of light, posed the simple question to himself. Why was he there?

The answer was nowhere near as clear cut as he would have liked. A faint hope that Brother Angelo might be in the *Cathédrale* too? Perhaps even now hiding in one of the many dark areas out of range of the projectors? It was possible – all things were possible. But was it likely? It was an eerie thought; the more so because as far as he could tell there was no one else about. Certainly nobody he could see or hear. There was no sign of the other visitor the girl at the cash desk had mentioned. He hadn't been aware of passing anyone. Whoever it was might well have left by now. A dozen people could have crossed his path and he would never have known. Looking around, shadows manifest themselves in unlikely places.

Deep down, Monsieur Pamplemousse began to wish he had been firmer with the *vétérinaire* and insisted on Pommes Frites' immediate discharge. Now filming had stopped, surely he would have welcomed a return to his old duties? Although, having said that, quite what he would have made of the present surroundings was hard to say.

The music swelled. It was modern, specially composed, loud, strident, synthetic; not to his liking, yet he had to admit it was somehow right for the setting. The rate at which the images changed increased with the volume; a never-ending montage of stained glass windows, of saints and ecclesiastical figures one after another, a riot of reds and blues and all colours of the rainbow. The overall effect as both sound and vision reached a crescendo was so intensely theatrical, he found himself unable to resist an overwhelming urge to take advantage of being on his own join and in; to hold his ears and shout out.

'Brother Angelo! Ron Pickles! *Avancez*! Come out! *Ici*! I know you are here!' His voice rose above the sound of the music.

Monsieur Pamplemousse never knew what hit him. There was a crash and a glancing blow across the back of the head sent him sprawling.

He lay where he had fallen for a moment or two, vaguely aware of a strange sound like the ticking of a myriad clocks echoing round the vaulted chambers. It was a moment or two before he came to his senses and realised that the house lights were on and that the noise was coming from the projectors as they recycled themselves for the next performance.

Climbing unsteadily to his feet, he looked up. Immediately above his head there was a steel bracket attached to the pillar. It supported a small platform for one of the projectors. There was a mark along the edge as though it had been struck by some heavy object. The metal was shiny where the paint had been removed. Glancing down he saw some splinters of wood on the ground. He rubbed his head ruefully. His senses were still spinning, but at least the bracket and the fact that he was wearing his hat had saved him from something far worse than a headache.

Monsieur Pamplemousse pricked two large potatoes several times with a fork and placed them on a piece of folded paper towel to absorb the moisture, then put them directly on the floor of the microwave oven. He checked once again with the cook book – it was as well to make sure – he had heard tales of potatoes exploding in microwave ovens, spattering themselves all over the inside. Reassured, he set the timer to 11 minutes, pressed the start button, and stood back.

Nothing sinister happened, so he began checking the rest of the shopping with his list. Butter, eggs, parmesan cheese, *asperge*, flour, *baguette, saucisson d'Arles* . . .

Already he was feeling better. The episode in the *Cathédrale* seemed like a bad dream. Nevertheless, it had left him feeling shaken. Cooking would be good therapy.

The pinging of the timer brought it all back. He couldn't think what had come over him. Shouting out had been an act of sheer bravado: a momentary mental aberration. Telling anyone else about his actions would be

119

embarrassing in the extreme. He certainly couldn't picture trying to explain to the local police what had happened. It made him blush even to think of it.

Taking the potatoes out of the oven, he halved them both and scooped out the middle from all four sections. Then he took a potato masher from the rack and beat the pulp until it was smooth. Adding around thirty grams of butter and an egg, he carried on beating. The heat of the potato caused the egg to cook slightly and helped thicken the mixture. Adding some flour, he carried on beating until it was firm enough not to stick to his fingers.

If there had been anyone else around in the cave he wouldn't have dreamed of behaving as he had. One thing was certain – it was the very last time he went on an expedition like that without Pommes Frites at his side. If Pommes Frites had been there to protect him it would not have happened. He should never have agreed to their being parted in the first place. It had been a moment of weakness on his part and now he was regretting it. For all he knew Pommes Frites could be thinking the same thing. The sooner their relationship was restored to normal the better.

He weighed out sixty grams of the parmesan cheese, grated it and added it to the mixture, beating it again. Then he added some pepper and salt and a pinch of nutmeg.

Leaving the mixture to cool, Monsieur Pamplemousse began preparing his first course – boiled eggs with *asperge*; the eggs lightly done so that he could dip the tips of the *asperge* into the yolk – having first coated them with melted butter, of course – and naturally having seasoned the eggs with pepper and salt.

Another thing was certain. If it had been Brother Angelo hiding in the cave – and he couldn't for the moment see any other reason for the unprovoked assault – then almost certainly he would have been well and truly scared away.

The table laid, Monsieur Pamplemousse put a large saucepan of salted water on the hob to boil, then spread some flour generously over the working surface above the base unit cupboard. Having first checked that his mixture had cooled sufficiently, he took a handful and rolled it into a long, thin sausage about two cm across. With a sharp knife he cut the sausage into sections, each one as long as it was wide.

Dipping a fork into the flour, he set about flattening the pieces, working each one with the prongs until resembled a sea shell.

The thing was, if it had been Brother Angelo, and if he had taken flight, where would he have gone to?

Adding the shells to the boiling water, he turned down the heat and left them to simmer for ten minutes or so. This was the tricky part; overcook them and they would become like curdled milk.

Perhaps it was as well Pommes Frites wasn't with him. He wouldn't take to all the preparations that were going into the meal. Waiting around for things to cook when he was hungry was not what he was best at.

Monsieur Pamplemousse wondered again about the things he had found in Brother Angelo's trailer. Daudet's *Letters from a Windmill in Provence* was an old English translation. It had been published in 1922 by a London firm – Arthur H. Stockwell. It looked as though it might well be a collector's item. If that were the case then Ron Pickles must have brought it with him. He certainly wouldn't have been able to buy it in Fontvieille. That suggested a more than passing interest in the subject.

The gnocchi had started to rise to the surface. Using a fish slice, Monsieur Pamplemousse removed the first batch from the water, allowing it to drain before arranging the shells in a buttered ceramic baking dish. Sprinkled with grated cheese and melted butter and baked in the oven until golden brown, they would, along with a green

121

salad, be a perfect accompaniment to the *saucisson d'Arles*.

And if Brother Angelo had been hiding out in the *Cathédrale*, was he also responsible for the various acts of sabotage on the lot? If so, why? For what purpose? Did he dislike Von Strudel so much? It couldn't be anything to do with money. When it came down to it, he must be getting paid a pretty hefty sum for doing very little.

As he put some more shells to boil, Monsieur Pamplemousse began to feel more relaxed; at least it had taken his mind off his headache. Rubbing the bruise with the back of a spoon had worked wonders. He poured himself a glass of wine, checked the cooking time for the asparagus, and set the microwave oven again. It was a whole new world. No liquid – cooking by weight – no loss of vitamins. He put the eggs on the hob to boil.

Doucette would not have approved of the pile of washing up in the sink. He had used up almost the entire armoury of saucepans, but then he usually did.

There was a knock at the door. It was not the sound he most wanted to hear.

'*Entrez.*' Monsieur Pamplemousse pressed the start button on the oven, then looked round.

It was Gilbert Beaseley.

It would have been churlish not to invite him in, but his heart sank nevertheless. He had been looking forward to eating on his own.

'*Ciao.*' Monsieur Pamplemousse's invitation was accepted with alacrity.

Beaseley looked around as he entered the kitchen. 'The Galloping Gourmet strikes again!' He peered in the saucepan. 'I see we're going all Italian.'

'*Gnocchi de pommes de terre* is a Provençal dish,' said Monsieur Pamplemousse. 'Even the name comes from this part of the world – "*inhocs*".'

'You learn something new every day. You're sure I'm not intruding?'

'On the contrary.' Putting a brave face on the situation, Monsieur Pamplemousse took two more eggs from the carton.

'You've heard about the business last night, of course?' Beaseley settled himself down in the dinette. 'I have to admit I slept through it all. I'm glad they didn't pick on my trailer. I suppose they must have been after souvenirs. I don't even know if there was anyone inside it or not.'

Monsieur Pamplemousse remained silent as he poured another glass of wine. He was perfectly happy to let the other make the running while he carried on with the cooking.

Beaseley took the glass from Monsieur Pamplemousse. 'You know what they're saying now? There's a rumour Ron's disappearance heralds the Second Coming. I suspect the Publicity Department of cashing in. They'll probably let it simmer away for a while on what they quaintly call the back boiler – dreadful expression – then they'll make an official announcement.

'Von Strudel is beside himself – his favourite position – "Dos zis mean ve hov to wait three days before ve see him again?" '

Monsieur Pamplemousse couldn't help smiling. It was a larger than life imitation, but true or not, he could picture it. The oven timer started to ping.

'You've no more news, I suppose?' said Beaseley.

Monsieur Pamplemousse made a grimace. 'I went back with Pommes Frites last night, but by the time we got to the cave it was too late. He picked up a scent inside the tomb, but it was impossible to follow – too many people had been trampling around. No doubt he has stored it away for future reference. All I got for my pains was a lecture from the *vétérinaire* for removing him without permission. He's supposed to stay in under observation for another day.'

'I expect the vet's lonely, poor chap,' said Beaseley.

'Apart from a few odd doves I doubt if he has any other patients.'

Monsieur Pamplemousse put a large knob of butter into the last remaining saucepan and ignited the gas. Then he removed the eggs from the saucepan and added two more before serving Beaseley. The *asperge* had lost none of its colour. One up to the microwave.

'It would be an odd twist of fate,' said Beaseley. 'If our hero really has undergone some kind of Heavenly metamorphosis.'

'Ron Pickles?'

'I must admit it isn't a name I would have chosen. Ron Pickles of Sheffield doesn't have quite the same ring to it as Jesus of Nazareth.

'The Anglican church has been making valiant efforts to be "with it" in recent years, but being "with it" is one thing . . . Ron Pickles reeks of desperation . . . Mind you, I don't trust Romans either. He could be in the pay of the Vatican.'

Watching the smoke rise from the butter as it began to melt, Monsieur Pamplemousse wondered whether or not to come clean about his morning adventure. He decided against the idea, at least until they were through the first course. Everything was happening at once, and the timing of the boiled eggs was critical to their enjoyment.

'Perhaps he has been spirited away.'

'Carted away more like it,' said Beaseley. 'Did you see the look on the face of some of those girls during the filming yesterday? Talk about wetting their knickers with excitement – those that had any on. Given half a chance they would have been up there with him.' He broke off a piece of *baguette* and spread butter over it. 'I say – this *asperge* is good. In England we like it white and thick. It comes from always wanting to cover things up.'

Monsieur Pamplemousse prepared the dish of gnocchi, sprinkled some grated cheese over the top, covered it with cling film and decided to take a chance on the oven timing.

He opened a bottle of red Domaine de Trèvallon from Eloi Durrbach. It was labelled Coteaux d'Aix en Provence, Les Baux. An anomaly of the French wine laws, since Aix and Les Baux were some hundred kilometres apart. Expecting it to taste of bauxite, he was pleasantly surprised.

'So you don't subscribe to the Second Coming theory?' asked Beaseley. 'On the third day and all that . . .'

Monsieur Pamplemousse shook his head. 'If I did I would have to say that Monsieur Pickles's sense of timing has deserted him.' It seemed a good moment to bring Beaseley up to date.

For once Beaseley heard him out without a single interruption.

'You think Ron's disappearance was engineered all by himself?' he said at last.

'I am sure of it.' Monsieur Pamplemousse rubbed the back of his head. 'Aided and abetted by someone who turned out the lights. It would only have taken him a second to get out of the cave by himself. The "rock" was only a prop. It weighed next to nothing.' He recalled calling Ron's name in the *Cathédrale*.' He paused. 'Since when I suspect he has been hiding out in the *Cathédrale d'Images*. That would explain why he made so many visits there and why his refrigerator was empty. He must have been building up a cache of supplies.'

'So our Ron is trying to opt out of everything,' mused Beaseley.

Monsieur Pamplemousse nodded. 'For whatever reason.'

'Who needs reasons?' Beaseley attacked the idea with enthusiasm. 'Oscar Wilde hit the nail on the head when he said that in this world there are only two tragedies. One is not getting what one wants. The other is getting it. Brother Angelo has had more than his share of getting what he wants – or wanted. He wouldn't be the first pop star to find it had all gone sour on him. It's not always the having that's fun – it's the getting. Imagine ending up with life being one long "farewell" tour – your fans growing older and older in front of your very eyes.'

The timer began to ping again as the oven switched itself off. Monsieur Pamplemousse removed the gnocchi. Golden brown they were not. Doucette's worst suspicions would have been confirmed. He turned the oven grill on to make amends and while he was waiting for it to heat up he sliced some *saucisson* into a thick Provençal pottery dish. By the time he had finished, the gnocchi had reached a satisfactory colour.

The *saucisson* had been air-dried for at least six months – or so the shopkeeper had assured him. Pork predominated – coarsely chopped, with hard back fat added, and the beef had been finely minced. It had been seasoned with garlic, ground black pepper and peppercorns.

'Delicious!' said Beaseley appreciatively. 'The poet Ponchon once wrote a work of some ninety-six lines in honour of a *saucisson d'Arles*. It sounded somewhat excessive. Now I understand why.' He dabbed at his lips with a paper napkin. 'How does anyone disappear?' he continued. 'I mean really disappear off the face of the earth.'

'You need to be dedicated. It isn't as easy as it might sound. We live in a sophisticated and increasingly computerised society. So many things are cross-referenced these days. So many people keep records.' Monsieur Pamplemousse pushed the dish towards Beaseley. 'First and foremost you need a new identity. That can be found in any churchyard. Every time there is a bad plane crash or a ship is lost at sea there are bodies which cannot be identified because officially they never existed. People don't really care who you are so long as you can prove you are who you say you are. If you plan to travel at all you will need a passport. If it is a stolen one you need to be sure it didn't belong to someone with a record. That can be arranged if you know the right people – at a price – but Brother Angelo could afford to pay.'

'How about things like bank accounts and credit cards?' asked Beaseley.

'Anyone can open a bank account. Credit cards are only a matter of time. Companies are only too anxious to dish them out these days. You would need to change your appearance. Again, that isn't too difficult. A new hair-style, a moustache and some plain glasses can work wonders. In the long term there is always plastic surgery.

'It is easier if you are very poor or very rich. The average person needs to work and on the whole they tend to gravitate towards the things they know how to do. Eventually life catches up with them. Their details get thrown up on a computer screen somewhere and questions are asked.

'Loneliness can be a problem. It isn't always as easy as it sounds . . . forsaking all that has gone before. Family . . . friends.'

'I doubt if he will be alone,' said Beaseley. '*Cherchez la femme*. It may show me up as a ghastly old-fashioned fuddy-duddy, but I bet whoever has been helping him is a woman. Someone familiar enough with the set-up to know which plug to pull to cause the maximum effect.'

'Mangetout?'

'You must be joking. You've heard them together. She would be another reason for disappearing.'

'The Swedish *au pair*?'

Beaseley shook his head. 'She may be very beautiful – if you like that sort of thing, but she's a bit gloomy. Miss Iceberg herself. I don't think I've once seen her smile. If you ask me there's someone else on the horizon.'

Monsieur Pamplemousse was reminded of his night visitor. He would remember her scent for some time to come. A potpourri of a perfume. And she had certainly been no iceberg. He poured some more wine.

'One thing's certain,' said Beaseley. 'If Brother Angelo

has done a bunk for good his sales will rocket sky-high.'

'You think so? Surely there's nothing so dead as last year's pop record. Or last week's, come to that.'

'Death establishes a permanent enshrinement. There will be no more, so what is left becomes infinitely more precious. The bad is forgotten, the good lives on. Especially if he's done a bit of stockpiling. Think of all the Jim Reeves hits there were after he got killed. Sixteen years after his death he was still able to command a single in the top ten. And take Elvis Presley. He died in 1977 and he's still a thriving industry. His memory is perpetuated in every possible way you can think of. Graceland gets nearly three-quarters of a million visitors a year. It's second only to the White House as the most visited home in the United States. Each year they have a contest of look-alikes. There's a torchlight procession to his old home during Death Week. It's virtually unstoppable.'

'You're not suggesting Presley is still alive?' enquired Monsieur Pamplemousse.

'Hardly. But there are those who are only too willing to believe that he is. Anyway, alive or dead, the best investment a pop star can make for his family is to keep back a few tapes which can be "discovered" after he's gone. If Ron really has opted out and he's played his cards right he could live in comfort for the rest of his life.'

They sat in silence for a while, each busy with his own thoughts. Monsieur Pamplemousse drained his glass, then wiped his plate clean with the last of the bread. Taking a cucumber, he cut it into large slices and put them on a plate at the bottom of the oven. Then he switched the timer to four minutes. According to Barbara Kafka it would remove all the odours.

'May I offer you some dessert?'

Beaseley shook his head.

'I have some fresh peaches. Sliced in half and sprinkled with sugar and a little lemon juice . . . steeped in

128

some Beaumes-de-Venise . . .'

'You're worse than Montgomery,' said Beaseley. 'Don't tempt me.'

'*Café.*'

'No, thank you. I must go. I have things to do. I've stayed too long as it is. I'm taking advantage of the natural break to do some work on my book. Besides, it isn't every day you find Les Baux closed to the public. It's too good an opportunity to be missed. I have reached the point in my narrative when Les Baux must have been at its best: a hundred years before Raymond de Turenne arrived on the scene. It's hard to picture it now, but in the thirteenth century it was a town of several thousand inhabitants; a highly formalised society – famous as a court of love – where troubadours composed passionate verses in praise of the ladies in return for a kiss and one of these.'

Feeling inside his jacket Beaseley produced a peacock's feather. 'One of nature's miracles. A thing of beauty – a joy for ever. My inspiration.'

He gave a bow. 'Good luck in your search for the truth. I will leave you with another thought for today: "If a man will begin with certainties he shall end in doubts, but if he will be content to begin with doubts he shall end in certainties." Not me, I'm afraid – Bacon.'

As Gilbert Beaseley disappeared through the door Monsieur Pamplemousse noticed for the first time that there were white marks on the back of his jacket. The kind of marks which might be acquired through leaning against a limestone wall? Not for the first time he decided that Beaseley was someone who needed watching. He had a disconcerting habit of playing his cards very close to his chest.

Long after the other had gone, Monsieur Pamplemousse sat lost in thought. One thing was certain. If it had been Brother Angelo in the *Cathédrale* he wouldn't have risked staying there. He would have moved elsewhere, possibly meeting up with his lady love at a pre-arranged *rendez-vous*.

Time and again he went through the other clues he had found in the trailer; Daudet's *Letters from a Windmill*, the tourist brochure for Fontvieille marking the Massif de la Sainte Baume in the guidebook, the book matches from the restaurant in Les Saintes-Maries-de-la-Mer. The three places formed a rough triangle on a map of the area . . . all were within relatively easy reach . . .

Halfway through tidying the kitchen the telephone rang. It was the *hospice*. The patient admitted in the early hours was asking to see him.

There was some confusion over their names. For some reason the girl at the other end had them transposed. It sounded urgent – more of a command than a request – so he didn't bother correcting her.

'*Oui*. Tell him I will be there as soon as possible . . .'

'*Oui*, that is true. He can be a little difficult . . .'

'*Oui, mademoiselle* . . .'

Glad of a diversion, Monsieur Pamplemousse reached for his car keys. It sounded as though the Director was beginning to feel better.

8
PATIENT PROBLEMS

The Director emitted a loud groan. 'Please do not think I am being ungrateful, Aristide, but I am hardly in the mood for *cerises* at the present moment.'

Monsieur Pamplemousse glanced around for a chair, but the room was sparsely furnished in the manner of other *hospices* he had visited over the years. Establishments where the kindness and dedication of the nuns who tended the sick necessarily took priority over the *meubles* department. Finding nothing suitable, he perched himself on the side of the bed.

'I am sorry, *Monsieur*.' He gazed at an embroidered figure of an angel hanging above the bedhead. 'It was difficult to know what to bring you. I had thought of flowers, but then it occurred to me that the pollen might bring on a sneezing fit, which I'm sure would be painful. Oranges are difficult to eat without getting sticky. You would probably not welcome the presence of biscuit crumbs between the sheets. Cherries seemed to be a good compromise. They are a clean fruit, easy to eat, and I am told the variety known as Bigarreau are particularly sweet and succulent at the moment . . .'

'I daresay,' the Director winced as Monsieur Pamplemousse reached across the bed in order to help himself from a brown paper bag and in so doing compressed the mattress causing it to rise on the side furthest away from him. 'However, if you will forgive my saying so, food is not uppermost in my mind. I did not drive all the way down to Les Baux only to end up in a hospital bed watching you eat cherries.'

Monsieur Pamplemousse took the point. 'Molluscs are not at their best during the summer months, *Monsieur*, otherwise I would have brought you some oysters. The ancient Romans set great store on their healing powers. Who knows? A kilo or two might even bring about some restoration of life in that part of your anatomy which I am told bore the brunt of last night's attack.'

The Director gave a shudder. 'Oysters are the very last thing I need, Pamplemousse.' He motioned despondently towards a large mound in the centre of the bed. 'I doubt if I shall ever feel the need to eat one again.'

He sighed. 'What am I going to tell Chantal when we retire for the night? She is not a demanding person, but neither does she lack powers of observation. Rather the reverse. She will be the first to ask why I have need of a cage to support the bedclothes above my nether regions. I am told it may be several weeks before I can dispense with some form of protection. I need a story, Pamplemousse. I need a good one and I need it quickly.'

'You could say you had your mind on other things, *Monsieur* – the departure of some rare species of bird for cooler climes, perhaps – and you accidentally walked into a bollard. It would accord with your injuries.'

'In the middle of the Camargue?' said the Director gloomily.

Monsieur Pamplemousse gazed out of the window. The *hospice* was on the outskirts of Arles and the Director's room afforded a view across the Grand Rhône to the city itself. The Pont de Trinquetaille was packed with traffic; lorries and cars nose to tail moving at a snail's pace. Arles was a notorious bottleneck. He could see the Amphitheatre in the distance and some way to the left of that the railway station.

He glanced back at the Director. 'It is strange to think, *Monsieur*, that we cannot be very far from the spot where Vincent Van Gogh cut off his ear in a fit of madness and presented it wrapped in paper to a prostitute called Rachel.'

The Director glared at him. 'That is a singularly unfortunate remark in the circumstances, Pamplemousse,' he boomed. 'I trust you are not suggesting I should follow his example. I must say that if the purpose of visiting the sick is to bring them courage and good cheer, then you are signally failing in your task.'

Monsieur Pamplemousse fell silent. He was doing his best, but when the Director was in one of his difficult moods he was an impossible man to please. He didn't envy the nurse on duty.

'I would have come sooner, *Monsieur*. However, when I telephoned early this morning I gathered you were in intensive care.'

'You gathered correctly,' growled the Director. 'I was in intensive pain as well. I am extremely lucky to be alive.'

Monsieur Pamplemousse reached across for some more cherries. They were too good to waste. 'I could hardly believe my eyes when I saw you go past my trailer last night. It was like watching a ship at sea. An ocean liner caught in a storm.

'Wave upon wave of undulating flesh passed by my window. A great tide of pubescent womanhood moving as one, moaning and groaning as though possessed of the devil. In the moonlight and with Les Baux silhouetted against the night sky, it reminded me of a Disney cartoon – something from *Fantasia* perhaps; the inevitability of Mickey Mouse as *The Sorcerer's Apprentice* coupled with Moussorgski's *Night on a Bare Mountain*.' Monsieur Pamplemousse looked around for somewhere to place his accumulation of stalks and stones and drew a blank. He settled for the top of a bedside cupboard. 'It would have made a wonderful series of photographs, but unfortunately by the time I had reloaded my camera your trailer had disappeared from view.'

The Director stared at him. 'You were reloading your camera, Pamplemousse?'

'It needed a faster film, *Monsieur*. Madame Grante would not have been pleased if she found I had wasted all thirty-six exposures, as I undoubtedly would have done had I used the reel which was already in the camera. Besides, it was Kodacolor and the scene cried out for black and white.'

'At a time like that you were worrying about whether to use colour or monochrome?' The Director sank back on to his pillow. The strain was clearly telling on him. 'Did it not cross your mind, Pamplemousse, to come to my assistance?'

'Certainly, *Monsieur*. That was my very first thought. Then it occurred to me to wonder what one person could possibly do against so many.'

A shudder ran through the Director's frame. It was quickly suppressed. A look of pain crossed his face. 'Please do not remind me, Aristide. For as long as I live I shall remember the moment when the trailer door burst open and that drug-crazed, sex-starved mob entered.'

'With respect, *Monsieur*, they may have been high on drugs, but from all I have seen I doubt if they were starved of sex. Appetites whetted beyond their control, perhaps . . .'

'Allow me to be the judge of that, Pamplemousse,' boomed the Director. 'I can still feel their hot breath as they descended on me, shouting and screaming, tearing off their garments, casting them right, left and centre. Those lascivious lips, those hands, searching, all the time searching. Fortunately their sheer weight caused the vehicle to fall over on to its side and I was able to seek refuge beneath some kind of wall cabinet. It was not a moment too soon. My pyjama jacket was in shreds; the trousers had been ripped from my body. I cannot think what possessed them.'

Monsieur Pamplemousse contemplated the Director. All manner of possible replies jostled for position on the tip of his tongue. He suppressed them. It must have been a terrifying experience; one he would have had no wish to undergo himself. The nearest equivalent in his own experience had been the time in St Georges-sur-Lie when he had been attacked by the girls of the Drum and Fife Band led by Miss Sparkling Saumur, but that had been nothing by comparison. On the other hand, there was a corner of his mind which couldn't help but ponder other aspects of the affair. Why the Director? What possible reason could there have been? Could it have had to do with something he had eaten earlier that evening? Some ultra powerful aphrodisiac he had accidentally stumbled upon. Something peculiar to the region. Perhaps, whatever it was had combined with the heat and the night air. Had he added a dab or two of XS before retiring? The Director was reputed to be partial to such bedtime extravagances. If it had been a field trial then it had succeeded beyond its maker's wildest dreams.

Suddenly realising he was being watched, Monsieur Pamplemousse pulled himself together. Speculation as to the reason for the Director's sorry state was a waste of time at this stage. The fact of the matter was it had happened. Perhaps Beaseley was correct in his assumption that the fans had simply been after souvenirs. If that were the case finding an occupied bed in what they must have mistakenly assumed to be Brother Angelo's trailer would have seemed like a Heaven-sent bonus.

'Undoubtedly it was a horrifying experience, *Monsieur*. There must have been three or four hundred females, all of whom had clearly totally lost control of themselves. Their emotions must have reached a peak and then snapped like a ship's hawser strained to breaking point. There was no stopping them.'

'Four hundred and twenty-three, Pamplemousse.' The Director assumed the self-satisfied air of a company auditor putting the final touches to the firm's annual accounts after an exceptionally prosperous year.

Monsieur Pamplemousse gazed at his chief with admiration. 'You were counting, *Monsieur*? The *journaux* put it at over 500.'

'You know as well as I do they always exaggerate,' said the Director. 'Editors hate untidy figures. Give a journalist an odd sum and he will immediately round it off in an upward direction . . .' He broke off. 'Did I hear you use the word *journaux*?'

Monsieur Pamplemousse corrected himself. 'The *journal*, *Monsieur*. So far it has only appeared in a local paper. One of their reporters happened to be passing at the time. It was clearly something of a scoop for him and he made the most of it. I was hoping to bring you a copy but unfortunately the first edition has sold out.'

'This is terrible news, Aristide. Publicity is the last thing I wish for.'

'It will be hard to avoid, *Monsieur*. The activities of a film company are always good copy and given the temporary closure of Les Baux – which I am told has given rise to a great deal of local discontent – any incident such as the one last night will be seized upon.'

'Pamplemousse, I charge you with making certain it goes no further.'

Monsieur Pamplemousse looked dubious. 'I will do my best, *Monsieur*. But it is the kind of story *Paris Match* would give their eye teeth for. They are almost bound to pick it up. Besides, if news about Brother Angelo's disappearance has leaked out – as I am sure it will have by now – they will be hot-footing it here anyway.'

He looked the Director in the eye. ' I have no doubt the Paris boys are on a plane bound for Marseille at this very moment. Those that aren't will be on the TGV.'

136

'Then you must intervene. They must be stopped at all costs.'

'Short of sabotage, *Monsieur*, I doubt very much if that will be possible. There is an hourly service at peak periods.'

There was a knock on the door followed by a rustle of cloth as a nurse in nun's attire entered the room. Monsieur Pamplemousse rose to his feet as she came towards them holding a thermometer in her right hand. Brushing past him, she thrust one end into the Director's mouth.

'Monsieur Pamplemousse, you are very naughty. We can hear your voice right at the other end of the corridor.'

Monsieur Pamplemousse gazed at the girl's back. '*Mademoiselle*, I hardly think . . .'

He was about to remonstrate in no uncertain terms – if anyone had been raising his voice it had been the Director – but he broke off as a gurgling noise issued from the depths of the pillow. For a moment or two it looked as though his chief was about to have a fit. His head was rolling from side to side: his eyes were large and imploring.

A fit? Or was he trying to convey some kind of message? Monsieur Pamplemousse waited for the answer. He was glad help was at hand. There was something infinitely reassuring about the unflustered way the nurse was handling the matter. Had he been there on his own he would undoubtedly have pressed the emergency call button.

'There now! Just as I thought.' She removed the thermometer and looked at it with professional disapproval. Her worst suspicions confirmed, she entered the figure on a chart at the end of the bed. 'I do not want to hear another word, Monsieur Pamplemousse,' she said severely. 'Otherwise I shall have to tell the Mother Superior.'

Turning away from the bed, she assumed her addressing of visitors tone. '*Cinq minutes*, *Monsieur*. That is all. *Cinq minutes*. Not a second more.'

As the door closed behind her, Monsieur Pamplemousse stared at the Director.

'*Monsieur* . . .'

The Director placed a finger to his lips. 'You heard
what the good lady said, Aristide. *Silence*. *Défence de
parler*.'

'*Monsieur*. Why did she call you Pamplemousse?'

Monsieur Pamplemousse had to admit that the Director
did have the grace to colour slightly.

'I was about to tell you, Aristide – just before the nurse
came in. When I was admitted here last night I was
delirious. I hardly knew what I was saying. The simple
fact is that when they asked me for my details your name
sprang to mind.'

'*My name, Monsieur*?' Monsieur Pamplemousse could
still hardly believe his ears.

'I could scarcely give them my own. A man in my
position has to watch out for these things, Aristide.
Recognition would be disastrous. It would undermine the
authority of *Le Guide*; an authority which I need hardly
remind you has been painstakingly built up over the
years. Our illustrious founder, Monsieur Hippolyte
Duval, would turn in his grave. That apart, there is
Chantal to be considered. She wouldn't give me a
moment's peace ever again.'

Monsieur Pamplemousse stared at him.

'What about *my* peace, *Monsieur*. Supposing Doucette
gets to hear?'

'She is used to your philanderings, Pamplemousse. It
would come as no surprise. One more escapade is neither
here nor there.'

Monsieur Pamplemousse reached for his hat.

Alarm was written across the Director's countenance.
'You are not going already?'

'You heard what the girl said, *Monsieur*. *Défence de
parler*.'

'Please, Aristide . . . Stay a few minutes longer.

There's a good *homme*. I have been thinking . . .'

'I, too, have been thinking,' said Monsieur Pamplemousse coldly. 'My thoughts tell me it is time I returned
to Paris. My work here is done, if indeed it ever began.
Such culinary advice as I was able to offer has been totally
disregarded. No one is in the slightest bit interested. I was
sent here under false pretences . . .'

'Aristide, I know you of old. Had I told you the real
reason why I wanted you to come down here, imagine the
fuss you would have made. You would have dreamed up
all manner of excuses. The truth is, when, over dinner, I
heard that subversive deeds were afoot, I volunteered
your services on the spur of the moment. I should have
consulted you first, of course, but the offer was accepted
with gratitude. I then found myself on the horns of a
dilemma. There was no going back.'

'We all have our problems, *Monsieur*.'

'Aristide, you cannot mean this. You cannot be serious.
You cannot abandon me. At any moment the reporters
may burst into this room. I am hardly in a state to defend
myself. They will be like a pack of wolves. There will be
photographers . . .'

'Are you suggesting, *Monsieur*, that I should by some
means or other spirit you away?'

'You know about these things, Aristide. There must be
somewhere I can hide . . . just for the time being . . .
until I am able to walk again?'

The Director looked around him desperately, as if
searching for inspiration. 'As I said a moment ago, I have
been thinking . . . on your way back to Paris why don't
you take your time. Pay a visit to Bocuse. Make a little
detour via Troisgros at Roanne. But before that there are
other three-Stock-Pot establishments *en route*. There is
Pic at Valence. I need hardly tell you . . .'

Monsieur Pamplemousse had a feeling of *déjà vu*. If it
was shared by the Director, there was no outwardly
visible sign. The conversation in his office only a few days

139

earlier might never have taken place. He hesitated. Deep down, now that his feeling of indignation had subsided, he knew there was no question of his not coming to the rescue. On the other hand it would do no harm to let the chief ramble on for a while. It would be interesting to see what other goodies he would dream up.

'There is a little restaurant north of Orange you could visit. I called in there myself on the way down. The *patron* is known locally as the King of the truffles. His concoctions, Aristide, are out of this world; omelettes which are *baveuse* in the *oeuf* department, but filled with great crunchy chunks of the noble fungus. He is also a compulsive buyer of wine from the Rhône valley. The only criticism one might level at him is that his list is too eclectic. It is overpowering in its vastness. It makes the choice difficult. But that is a fault on the right side. I would welcome your views.'

Monsieur Pamplemousse sighed. He knew when he was fighting a losing battle.

Sensing that capitulation was close at hand, the Director held out his hand. 'I knew you wouldn't let me down, Aristide.'

'Leave it with me, *Monsieur*. I will do my best.'

'I could not ask for more,' said the Director simply. 'And the troubles back at the location? You will look into those too?'

'I will look into those too, *Monsieur*.' He took the proferred hand. 'But first things first.'

They were only just in time. The door opened and the nurse entered. She looked at her watch. 'Your time is up, *Monsieur*.'

'I think possibly Monsieur . . . er . . . Pamplemousse needs his sheets changing.' It was hard to resist the temptation. 'He is very restless and he wants to look his best for the photographers when they arrive.'

'*Au revoir*, Aristide,' said the Director pointedly. 'I think you should hurry.'

'I shall be back, *Monsieur*. Rest assured, one way or another I shall return.'

'Tcchk! Tcchk!
  '*Sacré bleu*!
  '*Mon Dieu*! *Mon Dieu*!
  '*Un désastre formidable*!'

Carefully removing a pair of rubber gloves, Monsieur Pamplemousse placed them on the bedside table alongside the cherry stones which he had abandoned earlier in the day. Out of the corner of his eye he could see the Director visibly blanching. Insofar as cold sweat was metaphorically able to mix with calcium carbonate, his face had gone a chalky white. Enough was enough.

Monsieur Pamplemousse was also only too well aware that his every move was being watched by others in the room, albeit with the reverence accorded to those whose knowledge and experience by definition far outshone that of his audience, but he needed to be careful. So far everything had gone according to plan; it would be a pity to overplay his hand.

It was early evening before he had arrived back at the *hospice*. Glancing up at his reflection in the rear view mirror as he drove in through the gates, he'd had to admit that the time he had spent at the make-up desk in his trailer had not been wasted. Unable to locate Anne-Marie, it had been very much a do-it-yourself job, but he looked – and felt – ten years younger. A thin layer of Mehron 26A Tan Glow make-up had changed his skin tone and formed the base for other titivations. No more than an inch of shadow applied midway between his cheek and jaw bones had changed the shape of his face. A thin line of collodion applied to his forehead suggested a past accident, repaired perhaps by another master surgeon. Parting his hair on the wrong side had worked wonders. His natural greyness now looked becomingly premature. Distinguished was a word which sprang to mind.

Matching eyebrows and moustache provided the finishing touch.

Wardrobe had come up with a lightweight tropical suit and suitable accessories. Props had provided a pair of thick-rimmed plain glass spectacles. Both departments had been only to pleased to get their teeth into the problem – no questions asked. It helped break the monotony of waiting for something to happen. Work on the production had been brought to a temporary standstill. The local police had been much in evidence; taking statements, measuring wheel tracks, interviewing eyewitnesses. Brother Angelo was still nowhere to be found. The big test came when he found himself being interviewed for the second time in less than an hour by the same officer, who failed to recognise him.

Having parked his car as far away from the main entrance to the *hospice* as possible – apart from the fact that it wouldn't do for anyone to recognise it, a 2CV was hardly in keeping with his new role – he had taken the bull by the horns, relying on a peremptory manner to bluff his way through. Speed was the order of the day. 'Don't give the other side time to think,' his motto.

With a white gown billowing out behind, a stethoscope hanging loose from one of its pockets, Monsieur Pamplemousse couldn't help but wonder if he wasn't overdoing things slightly. Would an eminent surgeon dress in such a manner? Wouldn't he be more likely to arrive immaculately attired and with a beautiful secretary in tow? But he needn't have worried. The only reason the red carpet hadn't been rolled out was because his arrival had taken everyone completely by surprise, which was as he'd intended. Had he forewarned the *hospice* he was coming, they might have tried looking him up in some medical *Who's Who*.

Using the Director's own name had been an added touch. Monsieur Leclercq of the 16th arrondissement produced the desired effect. Say no more. It was an area

142

of Paris renowned for housing the *crème de la crème* of the medical profession. As an address, its very mention was an open sesame.

What he hadn't bargained on was the Director himself failing to penetrate his disguise. That needed to be rectified.

He turned away from the bed. 'This man must be operated on as soon as possible. Otherwise,' he made a suitable gesture to his audience. '*Amputé*!'

The Director's face went an even paler shade of white.

'Do not worry, *Monsieur*,' hissed Monsieur Pample-mousse.

'Do not worry!' repeated the Director. 'You use the word *amputé* about one of my most precious possessions and then you say "Do not worry". I demand a second opinion.'

Monsieur Pamplemousse's heart sank. 'The operation will need to be done in Paris,' he said, loudly and clearly for the Director's benefit. 'Away from here.'

'*Amputé*!' A man in evening dress who had clearly been called away from some important function turned to the Sister. 'Why was I not informed of this, Sister Agnes?'

'*Monsieur* . . .' The Sister was temporarily thrown off balance. 'It is the first I have heard . . .'

'*Silence*!' Hurriedly breaking into the conversation before it took a dangerous turn, Monsieur Pamplemousse hooked the hearing end of his stethoscope over the Director's ears. 'Keep very still, *Monsieur*.'

He turned to the others, 'An old trick. It keeps them occupied when delirium is setting in. Poor fellow. He is so overwrought he doesn't even recognise his old family surgeon, Monsieur Leclercq.'

Placing the business end to his lips he hissed the words 'It is I, Pamplemousse.' His words produced a satisfactory response. The Director gave a start and nearly fell out of bed. 'See, it works!'

'Now, you have some x-rays, I trust. Blood group confirmed? Measurements taken?'

The others exchanged glances. 'There has hardly been time, Monsieur Leclercq,' said Sister Agnes nervously. 'The doctor who has been attending Monsieur Pample- mousse is off duty and . . .'

'Tcchk! Tcchk!' Monsieur Pamplemousse was begin- ning to enjoy himself. 'I ask because it may be necessary to carry out a transplant.'

'A transplant! *Mon Dieu!*' A noticeable tremor of excitement ran round those present. One of the nurses crossed herself.

'You could carry out the operation here, *Monsieur*. Such an historic moment will help us gain valuable publicity for our *Amis du Hospice* fund-raising project. Doubtless you saw the board outside. If I may, I would like to be present while it takes place. Perhaps an article in the medical *journal* afterwards. With your permission, of course . . .'

'I am afraid that will not be possible,' said Monsieur Pamplemousse firmly. 'Utterly out of the question. To start with, the patient belongs to a rare blood group – *très, très rare*. Then there is the question of finding a suitable donor. Monsieur Pamplemousse is from the north. He is very particular about his lineage. He would not wish to be endowed with a Provençal attachment. Nor, I suspect, would Madame Pamplemousse be best pleased.

'I shall, of course, perform the operation myself. He must be transferred to Paris immediately.' Monsieur Pamplemousse looked at his watch. 'If he is not on his way within the hour I shall not be responsible for the consequences. The success rate, alas, is not high. Time is not on our side.'

Sister Agnes gave a tiny curtsy. '*Oui, Monsieur*. At once, *Monsieur. Je m'en occuperai.*'

'I trust you know what you are doing,' cried the Director as the others rushed out of the room leaving them on their own for the moment.

'*Monsieur*, have I ever let you down?'

144

'There is always a first time, Pamplemousse. Words like
amputé and transplant should not be treated lightly. I fear
the worst. I do not trust the medical profession. Did you
see the look in that man's eyes? The one in evening dress.
A frustrated butcher if ever I saw one. Doubtless he was
attending a local bullfight. He cannot wait to get me on
the slab.'

'Do not alarm yourself, *Monsieur*.' Monsieur Pamplemousse laid a soothing hand on the Director's shoulder. 'Everything is under control. I have arranged for you
to be admitted to a private hospital in Paris. It is an
establishment of the utmost discretion. They deal at
government level with all manner of problems, so they are
well used to the unusual.'

He felt inside the pocket of his gown and withdrew a
small brown envelope. 'I have taken the liberty of pur-
chasing a series of postcards particular to the region. They
depict various delicacies – *soupe au pistou, boeuf en
daube, salade noiçoise* . . . so they will not tie you down
as to exactly where you are staying. If you care to inscribe
them as though you are constantly on the move and
address them to Madame Leclercq, I will see they are
mailed at regular intervals. A short non-committal message or two along the lines of "Wish you were here", or
"Regret severe local storms have disrupted lines of com-
munication" will suffice. She need never know. In the
meantime . . .'

The door was flung open.

'Monsieur Leclercq . . . there is a private ambulance
leaving shortly for Paris . . . but it is meant for another
patient.'

'Then you must commandeer it!'

'*Mais* . . . it is an emergency case. He has only just
been admitted.'

'No "buts",' thundered Monsieur Pamplemousse. 'This
is equally a matter of life and death. I shall hold you
all personally responsible.' He held the door open. 'If

nothing is done I shall inform the minister . . . heads will roll.'

Following Sister Agnes out into the corridor, Monsieur Pamplemousse viewed the scene with satisfaction. The normal cloistered calm had vanished. He couldn't remember when he'd last seen nuns running. The rustle of their habits sounded like a flock of frightened birds taking to the air.

A man encased from head to foot in plaster was being whisked on a trolley from one room to another. It must be the emergency Sister Agnes had spoken of, for he heard the bleep of someone being paged. It sounded urgent. Any momentary pangs of conscience were quickly stifled. In this day and age someone would surely find a solution to the problem.

Porters scurried to and fro. Somewhere in the distance he heard a telephone ringing. No one was bothering to answer it. It had all the ingredients of a television serial at its most chaotic. The only thing missing was Von Strudel shouting '*Dummkopf*' through his megaphone. Given his presence, the scenario would have been complete.

Monsieur Pamplemousse moved to one side as two more porters headed his way pushing a trolley. They disappeared into the Director's room. Moments later they emerged.

The Director managed a wave as he shot past. 'You are a good fellow, Aristide. I shall not forget this.'

Monsieur Pamplemousse waited just long enough to make sure his chief wasn't being wheeled towards the operating theatre, then he paid his respects to the sister.

'*Chère* Sister Agnes, please ensure Monsieur Pamplemousse is well looked after. And beware of answering any questions from *les journaux*. In return I will see your kindness and efficiency does not go unrewarded. A little contribution towards your fund, *peut-être*?'

It was the least the Director could do in the circumstances.

★ ★ ★

Back at base Monsieur Pamplemousse turned off just
inside the main entrance and drove along a rutted path-
way towards the scene of the Director's downfall. The
trailer was still lying on its side. It looked sad and
abandoned. Someone from wardrobe must have made a
desultory attempt at retrieving the discarded garments,
for they were laid out in neat piles on a trestle table
awaiting collection. Using a window frame as a foothold
he climbed up on top of the trailer. The door was lying
open. He peered through the opening. The inside had
been stripped bare. Any thoughts he might have had
about retrieving the Director's belongings died a death.
There weren't any. The souvenir hunters had picked it
clean. He clambered unsteadily to his feet.

Closing the door was almost like putting the lid back on
a coffin. There was an air of finality about it.

It had been an automatic gesture; akin to straightening
the cutlery on an untidily laid table, no more. But as the
door fell shut he stared at it. There, right in front of his
eyes, was the answer to one of the questions uppermost in
his mind. The name board screwed to the top of the door
bore not the Director's name as he might have expected,
but that of BROTHER ANGELO.

Monsieur Pamplemousse stared at it for several seconds
while he absorbed the implications. It certainly explained
why the Director had been so disorientated the previous
evening and why the fans had descended on the trailer.

He knelt down and examined the name board more
closely. The slots in the screws used to fasten it to the
door showed distinct signs of having been tampered with.
The metal was shining through in places where the layer
of fresh paint had been penetrated.

Climbing back down off the roof, Monsieur Pamplemousse made his way back to his car. He was tempted to
use the telephone and ring his chief to tell him the news.
Then he thought better of it. The girl at the switchboard

might well listen in. Given all that was going on he wouldn't have blamed her.

Switching on the engine, he drove slowly back towards his quarters, scanning the track on either side as he went. He had only gone a matter of some twenty metres or so when he saw what he was looking for. Something silver gleaming in the scrub to his right. It was the end of a long screwdriver. Monsieur Pamplemousse picked it up by the middle of the blade and wrapped the handle carefully in his handkerchief. Paint still adhered to the business end.

His immediate assumption was that someone had done a straight swap of the Director's name plate and Brother Angelo's, but as he drew near the site he realised others had been tampered with too. His own name plate was now attached to the door of Mangetout's trailer. It was no wonder the Director had gone there by mistake. Familiarity bred contempt and the old hands probably never even bothered to look for their names any more. Why should they? Monsieur Pamplemousse had to admit he had stopped doing so himself. It had never occurred to him to check the name plate on his own door, any more than he had bothered to check the name on Brother Angelo's trailer when he'd broken into it. To compound the problem, when he reached Pommes Frites' trailer he discovered it bore the name of Gilbert Beaseley.

Someone had taped a message to the door. 'Hope I have done the right thing. Am a little confused.' It bore an illegible signature.

Monsieur Pamplemousse tapped on the door and waited a moment before trying the handle. It opened to his touch.

The expression on Pommes Frites' face when he saw who his visitor was made his previous performance by the Ark pale into insignificance. Unalloyed joy radiated from every pore as he jumped to his feet, scattering bowls of food and water in all directions.

Monsieur Pamplemousse responded in like vein. Words

148

were unnecessary. Recriminations would have been unthinkable; worse than the endless post-mortem of two bridge players raking over past mistakes. What had been done was in the past, and not up for discussion. A touch, a gesture, a lick, the wagging of a tail, a lingering pat, they said it all. Master and hound were as one again.

That fact clearly established, Pommes Frites stretched and wagged his tail in anticipation as he followed his master out of the trailer and back towards their rightful home. The signs were unmistakable. Clearly, there was work to be done.

9
DID HE FALL OR WAS
HE PUSHED?

Monsieur Pamplemousse set off with Pommes Frites shortly after breakfast the following morning. It was time he put his money where his thoughts lay. To 'put up, or shut up' as the Americans would say.

It was good to be together again. Together and on the open road. Pommes Frites patently felt the same way. You could tell by the way he was sitting. If Pommes Frites didn't want to go somewhere, then he always left Monsieur Pamplemousse in no doubt as to his feelings. Driving a 2CV with some fifty kilos or so of solid flesh leaning the wrong way every time you turned a corner was extremely tiring, not to say hazardous. Today he was behaving like a seasoned pillion passenger on the back of a motorcycle; swaying with the movement rather than against it.

With the canvas roof rolled back and the roar of the slipstream in their ears, life was as it should be; the horizon free for the moment of any unpleasant blemishes, the world their oyster.

Leaving Les Baux behind them, Monsieur Pamplemousse headed towards Fontvieille, anxious to put his theory to the test.

His feeling of euphoria was short-lived. The harsh world of reality soon made its presence felt. It was Sunday traffic at its worst. Caught behind a slow-moving coachload of schoolchildren, he turned on the radio. There was music, followed by a news bulletin: a catalogue of international woes. After the headlines came the local items. Pride of place was given to the latest happenings at the film location, but there was no mention of the Director. Sister Agnes must have taken his little talk to heart. Brother Angelo's mysterious disappearance, now officially admitted, dominated the talk. Speculation as to its possible religious significance was growing.

Monsieur Pamplemousse wondered idly if Beaseley had his radio on. He doubted it. When he'd tried ringing the other's number before leaving there had been no reply. Quite likely he was out early gathering material for his book.

There was an interview with a local Curé who cast cold water on the very idea of a Second Coming. God, he implied, moved in mysterious ways, but there were limits even to His degree of tolerance. Enlisting the aid of a pop star – an English one at that – was one of them. On the spot interviews with various locals produced a wide variation of views. Clearly there were those who would like to believe the worst – or the best, according to one's standpoint.

At least the Director was back in Paris by now. A second telephone call had confirmed his arrival there in the early hours of that morning.

Any hopes Monsieur Pamplemousse might have entertained about losing the coach in Fontvieille were quickly dashed. As they approached some traffic lights in the centre of the village the driver signalled a left turn. Monsieur Pamplemousse followed suit. Small faces gazed out of the rear window at Pommes Frites as they were tailed up a long pine-shaded avenue leading out of the village and on to the D33, then left again into a vast and crowded car park. There they waved goodbye as the coach peeled off and disappeared in a cloud of dust.

The picture in the guidebook which accompanied the

description of the windmill where Alphonse Daudet was reputed to have drawn the inspiration for his stories showed a circular stone building with a black pointed roof standing in splendid isolation on top of a small hill to the south of the village. A cypress tree framed the left side of the picture, whilst a solitary goat to its right directed the viewer's eye towards the great wooden sails of the mill itself. The tips of two small patches of white cloud in the top corners of the picture added symmetry, breaking up an otherwise azure blue sky. There was not a human being in sight. It was a peaceful scene, one which any writer would have yearned for. An ideal spot for a lover's meeting.

As Monsieur Pamplemousse drew in between two coaches, one taking on a load of old-age pensioners, the other in the act of filling the vacuum left by the departure of another, it struck him that the guidebook's picture was either a very old photograph or whoever was responsible had been singularly fortunate in his choice of days. There were people as far as the eye could see, people preparing for a picnic, people playing games, people taking pictures of other people. The hill on which the windmill stood was alive with antlike figures. There was no sign of the goat. It must have long since given up in disgust.

Monsieur Pamplemousse decided to follow its example. Without even bothering to get out of his car, he bade farewell to the Moulin de Daudet and headed back the way they had come, resolutely turning left in the village on to the road to Arles.

Despite his momentary disappointment, it was what detection was all about; the piecing together of unrelated scraps of information – discarding one, picking up another, like pieces in a jigsaw puzzle. Completing the final picture was often a matter of trial and error. That and painstaking application. If the ticket stubs to the *Cathédrale* had turned up trumps there was always a possibility one of the other clues might do likewise.

A member of an animal rights group was holding forth on the radio, speaking on behalf of the South East Asian civet, prized for its overpowering odour of narcissus and much used by the perfume industry as a fixer and blender, but when questioned about Brother Angelo's disappearance he denied all knowledge.

A flower grower from Grasse declared that even if it wasn't the Second Coming, it was still an act of God. Revenge on the profiteers in Paris who kept forcing down prices and depriving people of their livelihood.

Arles was stiflingly hot and the traffic was at a standstill. It was a classic man-made bottleneck. Posters advertised a week's programme of bullfighting, which couldn't help matters. The city looked full of sightseers. Cafés and restaurants lining the main through-road were already crowded. The holiday season was well underway.

A little way out of Arles he turned off the main road in order to make a detour round the Étang de Vaccarès.

The Camargue was as he remembered it – vast and flat; all 800 square kilometres of it. Driving past beds of reeds and rushes, he could already taste the salt in the air. There were pine trees shaped like parasols, acres of furze bushes, and rice fields everywhere; it was the big new industry. Thick cypress hedges acted as windbreaks. *Promenades à Cheval* signs proliferated; so much for the famous wild horses.

They passed a little cottage with a wooden sabot hanging by the front door. In the old days it would have been ready to receive an anonymous token of friendship from any passer-by who felt so inclined – an egg, a posy of flowers, an orange; now it had most likely been put there simply as a tourist attraction. There were roses in the garden, growing to a height undreamed of further north.

Discounting all the wild theories on the radio, the inescapable fact was that Ron Pickles, alias Brother Angelo, had disappeared without trace. The more he thought about it, the more he went over his conversation with Beaseley, which had helped crystallise his own thoughts, the more he felt sure he was right. Apart from Beaseley, he had passed on his suspicions to no one. But knowing something deep down inside was a world away from proving it to be true.

The vast Étang came into view. It wasn't hard to imagine the furore the film company must have caused when they turned up intending to part it. At certain times of the year they might have got more than they bargained for. According to the guidebook, waves could reach a height of a metre or more.

He spotted a whitewashed, thatched *gardien*'s *cabane* nestling amongst some tamarisk trees. Built with a rounded rear and a tiny opening at the front to provide shelter from the Mistral, it would be equipped with a fireplace and everything needed to hold out for days at a time. In theory it would be an ideal hiding place for anyone on the run, but in practice the reverse would almost certainly be true. The Camargue was still a relatively unpopulated area. Anything the slightest bit out of the ordinary would be spotted immediately.

A brick-red patch in the water resolved itself into a group of flamingoes. One leg tucked beneath their plumage, they stood erect on their remaining limb as they busied themselves over an early lunch. Beaks plunged deep into the mud in search of worms and insect larvae and whatever else of interest might be lurking beneath the surface.

Monsieur Pamplemousse brought his attention back to Ron's disappearance. He had lain awake most of the night turning the problem over and over in his mind. It seemed to him that Beaseley's theory of *cherchez la femme* was the most likely. Ron must have had an accomplice and given his reputation it was more than likely to be female.

It certainly wasn't his agent. He was going around giving a passable imitation of the man who had lost the goose that laid the golden egg, and his fears sounded genuine.

And if Ron had fled the *Cathédrale*, where would he have gone to? Presumably somewhere not very far away. He'd left it too late to try and leave the country – at least for the time being. From all the coverage he had received everybody would be on the lookout for him.

If that were the case, then it would need to be somewhere pre-planned where he could meet up with his girl Friday when the coast was clear.

Daudet's windmill had been a disappointment, that he had to admit. Browsing through the guidebook at three o'clock in the morning it had looked an ideal rendezvous for a romantic meeting.

A buzzard on a reconnaissance mission flew high overhead, keeping a watchful eye on the passing scene. The flamingoes took to the air in a perfect V-formation.

Monsieur Pamplemousse glanced at his watch, wondering if he had time to stop and take a picture, but it was gone eleven-thirty. By rights they should be in Les Saintes-Maries-de-la-Mer.

At least they were making better time than Van Gogh. One June day in 1889 it had taken the painter five hours to make the journey by *diligence* from Arles. Including stops, Monsieur Pamplemousse in his *Deux Chevaux* had taken just under an hour. There was one great difference. After his journey Van Gogh was able to write to his brother, 'I walked one night along the deserted beach by the sea . . . It was beautiful.'

The pleasure of walking along a deserted beach was one which they were clearly not destined to share. Monsieur Pamplemousse's heart sank as he caught sight of an arrow pointing to an out-of-town car park. Ignoring the sign, he took a chance and followed one marked *Centre Ville*. Luck was with him. He found an empty space on a pedestrian crossing, and from there fought his way down towards the sea front and the old fortified church, built to commemorate the landing of Mary Magdalene after she had been cast adrift from the Holy Land. It was number two on his itinerary.

Place de l'Église was full of gypsies; the girls, dark-eyed and proud, pushed their way in front of the passers-by, almost daring them on pain of unmentionable future disasters to say no to having their fortune told. Any one of them, hearing his story, would probably have told him he was wasting his time. Anywhere less suitable for a clandestine meeting would be hard to imagine. He left Pommes Frites to wait while he went inside the church.

The one-franc coin Michelin advised him to have ready to feed into a coin operated light switch was redundant. The church was packed. There was nothing for it but to join the shuffling crowd of half-naked sightseers waving their video cameras to and fro like so many hosepipes.

It was hard to tell what they were thinking: a pause to see the fresh water well inside the nave at the far end, down into the crypt for a momentary glimpse of the statue of Sarah, patron saint of the gypsies, up again past a side altar with its model of the legendary boat, and suddenly he was outside again, inexorably ejected like the cork from a champagne bottle.

Pommes Frites had a faraway look in his eyes. He could have been dreaming once again of a penthouse kennel in Beverly Hills, or shopping at Cartier for a diamond encrusted collar. Monsieur Pamplemousse gave him a consoling pat. Mary Magdalene would have sympathised. She would have turned round and gone straight back to Palestine. Although in truth Pomme Frites' preoccupation had more to do with a gnawing feeling in his stomach than with his immediate surroundings.

The Cinema Le Camargue down by the harbour was showing an old Von Strudel film. A children's carousel on the other side of the road was doing a better trade.

It was as they were making their way slowly back to the car along an avenue Frédéric Mistral awash with souvenir shops, bars, cafés and restaurants, that Monsieur Pamplemousse remembered the matchbox he'd been carrying in his pocket. There was no point in leaving Les Saintes-Maries-de-la-Mer without exploring all the possibilities.

Le Croissant d'Or turned out to be a Chinese restaurant. It was a card of sorts, but not exactly the one he'd been expecting. Hardly the ace of trumps.

After the blinding sunlight, the inside looked distinctly gloomy. Even the bamboo had been painted black. A bead curtain made of old Coca Cola crown tops separated the kitchen from the main eating area. An unseen loud-speaker was emitting strains of what sounded like an oriental version for Chinese wood block and crash cymbals of 'I Did it My Way'.

Monsieur Pamplemousse chose a pavement table. Perhaps Ron, brought up on a diet of Chinese take aways in his native Sheffield, had been drawn to the restaurant on a wave of nostalgia – or desperation. He was beginning to feel that way himself.

Pommes Frites eyed his bowl of bean-shoots with a look of distaste bordering on downright suspicion; aware perhaps, with that extrasensory perception given to canines, that in other circumstances, in other climes, he might well have found himself featuring on the menu as an integral part of lunch 'C' – (*six personnes min.*). It was not what he'd had in mind while he'd been waiting outside the church.

Lunch was a hurried affair – the Chinese habit of bringing everything at once was not without its merits, but even so, by the time they had finished the restaurant was full. Monsieur Pamplemousse called for *l'addition* and mentally crossed it off his list.

Leaving Les Saintes-Maries-de-la-Mer by a back road, he headed for the car ferry near the mouth of the Rhône. It would be better than driving back to Arles and risking getting snarled up in the traffic again.

It was not the best idea he had ever had. There was a

long queue of like-minded drivers for the double-ended, drive on drive off boat, and it was late afternoon before they eventually arrived at their last port of call. Set high up in the steep northern face of La Sainte-Baume Massif, it was the cave where Mary Magdalene was reputed to have spent her last thirty-three years, and the one remaining place marked in Ron's guidebook.

As he parked his car, Monsieur Pamplemousse recognised the coach he'd followed into Fontvieille earlier in the day.

From where he stood it was impossible to see beyond the first hundred metres or so of the stony path which led up to the cave. It disappeared into a forest of huge trees – beech and lime and maple – rising majestically out of an undergrowth thick with holly and ivy.

He consulted *Michelin*. They quoted an hour on foot there and back. Another way of putting it was more likely to be an upward trudge of three quarters of an hour plus fifteen minutes to come back down again.

Glad of a chance to stretch his legs, Pommes Frites ran on ahead as they set off up the path. The first of the kamikaze mosquitos arrived almost at once. They were followed by a swarm of madly persistent flies. Halfway up they met an old lady sitting on a rock, awaiting the return of her family who were making the final assault. Monsieur Pamplemousse was sorely tempted to join her. Pommes Frites paused long enough to slake his thirst from a fresh water spring.

The path began doubling back on itself concertina fashion. Voices assailed them from all sides as schoolteachers dressed in suitable shorts led their chattering flocks on what was probably an oft-repeated end-of-term outing.

Steps carved into the sheer rockface came into view, followed by a door leading to the Sanctuary. There were signs asking for silence; others were marked NO FLASH and CHIENS INTERDITS. None were having much effect.

159

Predictably, it was a repeat of everything that had gone before. The inside of the vast semi-circular cave was packed with visitors. It was cold and it looked as though it was permanently wet. The only dry place visible in the flickering light from the candles was in a cavity behind the altar. It contained a recumbent statue commemorating the thirty-three years Mary Magdalene had spent there in solitude.

Monsieur Pamplemousse paid his respects and left. Ignoring a souvenir shop run by the Dominicans, he rejoined Pommes Frites on the balcony. The view from a thousand metres up was magnificent; the mountains in the far distance had a mauve haze from the fields of lavender. But he wasn't there for the view.

As an exercise in detection it had been a total disaster. In truth, romantic notions arrived at under cover of darkness seldom lived up to their promise next day. A feeling of dejection came over Monsieur Pamplemousse as he made his way down the steps, past a bronze Calvary and out through the gate to begin their downward trek. It had been a totally wasted expedition.

Taking it slowly to avoid catching up with a crowd of schoolchildren, he found himself wondering how the Director was getting on.

'As well as could be expected,' according to the Sister. That probably meant he was feeling sorry for himself. If he knew he'd been the innocent victim of a practical joke he would have felt even more upset. Or was it a joke? One of Von Strudel's 'bugginks'. Swapping two name boards might have been someone's idea of a bit of harmless fun. Moving four around was taking a joke a little too far. Six smacked of some deeper reason.

At least his chief was safely tucked up in a mosquito-free bed. He didn't know how lucky he was.

Monsieur Pamplemousse suddenly felt cut off from things. Paris seemed a long way away, remote and

160

eminently desirable, even though half the population would have fled to the sea.

Perhaps by the time he and Pommes Frites got back to Les Baux there would be some news. Ron might even have reappeared. Maybe it was all a publicity stunt; a gigantic Bible-inspired hoax. If that were so his time in hiding must be almost up.

Alone in his trailer, the memory of his night-time visitor still disturbingly fresh in his mind, it had been all too easy to arrive at a romantic answer. Beaseley would have embroidered it in cinematic terms; music reaching a climax as the two lovers walked towards each other in long shot before meeting in a passionate embrace. Cut to BCU. Hold for the final chords. Dissolve. Credits superimposed over a shot of the windmill.

Monsieur Pamplemousse stopped dead in his tracks as he realised there was a fatal flaw in his reasoning. He was allowing his heart to rule his head.

The girl who had entered Brother Angelo's trailer the night he was there must have been a regular visitor. She'd had a key and she knew her way around in the dark. Presumably she hadn't even bothered checking the name on the door. What was more, she hadn't been at all taken aback to find the bed occupied. Her immediate reaction had been one of pleasurable surprise rather than shock – her clothes had been discarded and she had climbed into bed without a second's hesitation – until she realised all too late the occupant wasn't who she'd expected it to be, when she'd fled like a frightened rabbit. The inescapable conclusion was that it must have been someone who was not only on intimate terms with Brother Angelo, but knew he was still in the area; hence the lack of surprise at finding him there.

If that were so, lovers' trysts as such were probably the last thing on their minds. Whoever it was would most likely stay put until the unit broke up rather than arouse suspicion.

161

Monsieur Pamplemousse's feeling of depression mounted as he and Pommes Frites climbed into his car and they set off on the homeward journey. Depression combined with a vague feeling of unease that was hard to rationalise.

The news on the radio was mostly about traffic jams, and even via the autoroute, dusk was already gathering by the time they reached Les Baux and checked in at the gate. Monsieur Pamplemousse drove straight to his quarters, parked the car, and did what he should have done at the beginning of the day; what he certainly would have done had his mind not been full of romantic notions. He took the screwdriver out of a drawer where he had left it and offered it to Pommes Frites. Pommes Frites gave the handle a thoughtful sniff, registered the information and fed it into his computer. Recognition dawned almost immediately. He looked enquiringly at his master.

'So?' he appeared to be saying, 'what are we waiting for?'

Monsieur Pamplemousse responded by opening the door of his trailer and standing clear.

Pommes Frites paused for a moment on the top step, then he set off at a steady pace with Monsieur Pamplemousse hard on his heels.

They went past each of the other trailers in turn with hardly a second's pause. First the front row and then in and out of the ones which were scattered behind. It wasn't until he had finished his second confirmatory tour of inspection that Pommes Frites came to a halt and sat waiting for further instructions. Monsieur Pamplemousse had to confess to a feeling of disappointment as he registered the name on the door. It was not what he had expected to see. Either Pommes Frites had done the unheard-of thing and made a mistake, or yet another of his theories had bitten the dust.

He was about to retrieve the screwdriver when he heard his name being called and turned to see Montgomery –

162

Von Strudel's chef – hurrying towards him.

'Monsieur Pamplemousse. Monsieur Pamplemousse, I have been looking for you everywhere. Have you not heard?'

Monsieur Pamplemousse gave a non-committal grunt. 'Pommes Frites and I have been away all day. Something has happened?'

'Monsieur Beaseley. His body has been found at the foot of the cliff.'

'The cliff? What cliff?'

'The one where the old castle once stood. The highest point in Les Baux.'

Monsieur Pamplemousse felt slightly sick. It was the spot where the sadistic Raymond de Turenne had made after-dinner sport of watching prisoners being hurled to their death – not far from the cave where Brother Angelo had vanished. Beaseley would have fallen more than 250 metres on to the rocks below. Death would have been instantaneous, but the moments before must have seemed endless.

'He has been identified?'

'There is no doubt.' Bernard hesitated. 'We shall miss his practical jokes. His whoopee cushions, his toads in the bed . . .'

Monsieur Pamplemousse gave a wry smile. 'His exploding stoves . . . his sand in the camera . . . his *savon d'agneau* when they were filming the Last Supper . . .'

Montgomery shook his head. 'No, those things were not the work of Monsieur Beaseley. There was no real harm in him. He once told me he caught the habit when he worked in a joke factory. Someone else must have been responsible. Someone who wanted to delay the production.'

He wiped his hands in a cloth. 'I must go. Herr Strudel will be looking for me. But I thought you should know.'

'*Merci*.' Monsieur Pamplemousse felt infinitely sad. It didn't seem possible. As always, there were so many things left unsaid; so many questions he should have asked. Now it was too late.

At least Beaseley had lived to see his name written in large letters on the door of a Hollywood-style trailer. It was fame of a kind, the next best thing to having it up in lights. But then, so had he; so had the Director.

Suddenly, he realised what he was thinking. He must be getting old – or tired – tired by all the driving.

The door Pommes Frites had led him to certainly bore the Director's name, but assuming no one had restored the sign boards to normal, the trailer was the one which had belonged to Brother Angelo.

If Pommes Frites had got it right, then it raised all sorts of questions. Following Montgomery's line of thought about the more bizarre acts of sabotage, why would Brother Angelo wish to delay the completion date?

And if he was becoming more and more desperate – desperate enough to have lashed out in the *Cathédrale* when he thought he'd been cornered, could he – either accidentally or on purpose – have been responsible for Beaseley's death?

Monsieur Pamplemousse's feeling of elation was short-lived. It was all pure conjecture on his part; conjecture based on circumstantial evidence. None of it would stand up in court for a second.

What had Beaseley's last words to him been? 'If a man will begin with certainties he shall end in doubt, but if he will be content to begin with doubts he shall end in certainties.'

Doubts Monsieur Pamplemousse had plenty of, but although certainties were beginning to take shape, they were still very thin on the ground. None of them took him the slightest bit further forward in the most important factor of all: locating the missing Brother Angelo, without whom nothing could be proved anyway.

10
THE RESURRECTION

It ended as it had begun, in Parc Monceau in the 8th *arrondissement* of Paris. Almost three months had elapsed since Monsieur Pamplemousse's last visit. Paris was back at work, and in a way it was both a voyage of nostalgia and a treat for Pommes Frites.

Work of a kind was the reason why Monsieur Pamplemousse found himself one autumn morning strolling in leisurely fashion down the avenue Montaigne accompanied by the Director. Each of them was carrying a black imitation-leather valise bearing the motif XS in gold letters on the side, for they had been to a private screening of the perfume commercial prior to its release.

After the vintage Krug champagne, the speeches, the overpowering chicness of beautiful hostesses, the plethora of congratulations – everyone received their share of praise, from the head of the perfume company to the commissionaire on duty at the projection studio – it was good to be outside again breathing comparatively fresh air. Names like Dior, Vuitton and Jean-Louis Schrerrer dripped expensively off buildings on either side of the tree-lined avenue.

'A triumph, would you not say, Pamplemousse?'

'Immaculate, *Monsieur*. Miraculous in its way.'

'I understand plaudits from various religious bodies around the world are arriving hourly. Doubtless you noticed there was a sprinkling of purple cassocks present this morning. It is amazing what can be achieved with judicious editing.'

Monsieur Pamplemousse had to agree. The proof of the pudding was in the eating and the end result was a work of art. Tasteful. Quite surprisingly moving in places. It was hard to picture anyone taking offence. A *Palme d'Or* at next year's Festival of Commercials was assured.

Pommes Frites' big moment came fairly early on during the flood. Seen in tight close-up, the expression on his face as he watched the Ark disappearing into the horizon drew a spontaneous round of applause. There was hardly a dry eye in the house.

Monsieur Pamplemousse found himself wondering what the reaction would have been had the audience witnessed the true cause of Pommes Frites' consternation – the collapse of the *papier mâché* palm tree.

'At least we can say we were in a film directed by Von Strudel,' said the Director, breaking into his thoughts.

'Along with Mangetout . . .'

'. . . and Brother Angelo.'

'You didn't think the make-up was a little over the top?' asked the Director anxiously.

'I think it was exactly right, *Monsieur*. And the lighting was superb. As for the casting – it was brilliant in its way. There was a kind of spiritual quality about his performance which was quite the reverse of all one had feared. And the fact that he disappeared before the final scene didn't matter at all. They must have amassed so much material in the earlier shots every eventuality was covered. Most of it was in close-up anyway, and the long shots were so brief you would never know it was a stand-in. Perhaps Eisenstein was right. One doesn't need actors . . .'

The Director clucked impatiently. 'I wasn't referring to Brother Angelo, Pamplemousse. I was thinking of my own appearance; the moment, albeit brief, when I was caught in the eye of the camera. You noted it, of course?'

The Director was clearly excited at having seen himself preserved on celluloid. No doubt for many weeks to come there would be breaks in the conversation at dinner parties while guests were forced to watch television commercials between courses.

'Although I say it myself, it is not hard to spot me.'

Hardly surprising, thought Monsieur Pamplemousse, since the Director was the only one looking towards the camera. He wasn't actually waving, but like the classic Hitchcock shot of the man who kept staring straight ahead at Wimbledon when all those around him were following the ball, once seen there was no taking your eyes off him. It was a wonder they had left it in. Perhaps they thought it added a touch of mystery. Speaking for himself, Monsieur Pamplemousse was glad his merging with the crowd had been rather more successful. All the same, the Director was right. They could have ended up like so many thousands of others – as out-takes on the cutting-room floor.

'I once played Robespierre in a school play,' mused the Director. 'Did you know he invented *mayonnaise*?'

'It was kitchen-sink drama, *Monsieur*?' asked Monsieur Pamplemousse innocently.

The Director glanced at him suspiciously. 'No, it was not, Pamplemousse,' he said gruffly. 'It was set at the time of the revolution. I mention it in passing merely as a matter of interest.'

They walked together in silence for a moment or two. A van bearing the letters XS on its side passed them.

'That was a bad business at Les Baux after I left,' said the Director. 'What do you think happened to that poor fellow? Lost his footing, I suppose.'

Monsieur Pamplemousse gave a non-committal grunt. It was a subject he still didn't feel like discussing.

'And what about Brother Angelo? They never found a body. No one ever claimed responsibility. I am glad the

"Second Coming" theory was thoroughly discredited. That would not have been good news.'

'It served its purpose,' said Monsieur Pamplemousse. 'Things could hardly have worked out better for the perfume company. All that free publicity for XS has acted as a teaser for the real thing.'

The Director gave him a sideways glance. 'Are you suggesting it was a put-up job?'

Monsieur Pamplemousse shook his head. 'Certainly not on the part of the perfume manufacturers. Nor the film company.'

'What then? If you are suggesting Brother Angelo spirited himself away, I do not see how he could have done it. The whole of the police force were looking for him at one point. The *journaux* . . .'

'One knows it is not possible to make an elephant vanish into thin air, *Monsieur*, but magicians do it every day. In his own way, with his stage act, Ron Pickles was something of an illusionist. He knew it was all a matter of timing. That, and some kind of distraction which would cause attention to be diverted elsewhere at the *moment critique*.'

'The turning off of the lights . . .'

'*Exactement*. For a few seconds everyone was looking everywhere but at the mouth of the cave. It was all he would have needed.'

'But why give up a successful career?' said the Director.

'The death – or in this case the disappearance – of an artist creates an entirely new set of values. Suddenly everybody realises the well has dried up, so the remaining water becomes more and more precious. If someone is lucky enough to find a hidden cache, their fortune is assured. Suppose one were to stumble across a collection of paintings by Monet. Or even a few sketches . . . a Mozart symphony . . .'

'They are hardly in the same category, Aristide.'

'Perhaps not in your eyes, *Monsieur*, but tastes vary. It

is over twenty years since Jim Morrison died in a Paris bath from a heart attack brought on by drugs and alcohol but his tomb in the Père Lachaise cemetery is rarely without its circle of worshippers. They would give anything for some tangible reminder.'

'Surely it is still preferable to be free to go anywhere one cares to choose rather than to renounce everything?'

Monsieur Pamplemousse was suddenly reminded of Beaseley's quotation.

'In this world there are only two tragedies, *Monsieur*. One is not getting what you want. The other is getting it.'

'That is a very shrewd remark, Aristide.'

'Unfortunately, *Monsieur*, an Irish writer thought of it first – before he, too, ended up in the Père Lachaise.'

They reached the point where the Director had parked his car.

'I haven't thanked you properly for coming to my assistance, Aristide. I don't know what I would have done without you.'

'There is no need to thank me, *Monsieur*. I only did what I thought was right at the time. I am glad it all worked out.'

While the Director felt for his keys, Monsieur Pamplemousse posed a question he had been dying to ask. 'You have had no problems *chez* Leclercq?'

'All is quiet on the distaff side,' said the Director. 'Ominously so, I thought for a while, but there is no knowing with women. So far I do not think Chantal has even noticed the extent of my indisposition. If she has, then she has passed no comment. She accepted my story without hesitation.'

'Your story, *Monsieur*?'

'The one about walking into a bollard. Once again, I have to thank you, Aristide. I simply transferred the location to Marseille. It struck me as being rather more believable. I'm sure it happens there all the time to drunken *matelots* reeling back to their vessels after dark.'

Monsieur Pamplemousse found himself hoping the Director hadn't embroidered his tale too much; something he was apt to do at times. He might well find himself in for a rough time at a later date when his wife discovered he had taken part in a perfume commercial. Questions were bound to be asked.

'And you, *Monsieur*. You are feeling better?'

'Much better, thank you, Aristide. As you can see, I am able to do without crutches for days at a time. Only when there is rain in the air do I feel certain twinges. I have been giving a lot of thought to the question of a transplant. Not serious consideration, you understand – who knows what problems might be unleashed? But it has kept me awake a good deal. The imagination has run riot.

'One thing is very certain, Aristide. Misfortunes of any kind have a sobering effect. None more so than in the world of medicine. It is always possible to see people worse off than oneself.'

'That is true of hospitals everywhere, *Monsieur*.'

'I wasn't thinking so much of the hospital,' said the Director. 'Although, as you said at the time, there are a lot of unusual cases there. It is incredible the things that some people in the highest echelons get up to. I could hardly believe my eyes – or my ears.

'No, I was thinking more of the poor man who shared the ambulance with me on my journey to Paris. Even now, I shudder to think what could possibly have happened to him. It made my own troubles seem minor by comparison. Swathed in bandages from head to foot like an Egyptian mummy. He didn't utter a word all the way there. Several times I tried to engage him in conversation in the hope of lightening his burden, but he seemed not to wish to talk.

'The nurse with him was equally reticent. It was strange. I could have sworn I'd seen her somewhere before. She pretended not to speak any known tongue, although she seemed to communicate very readily with the driver when we reached their destination. There was a dreadful commotion as they entered the building – something to do with getting the stretcher jammed in the lift doors. All hell broke lose. There was a crash and I heard a bleeper going as someone called for assistance. The *concierge* was either asleep or on holiday along with the rest of Paris. One can't rely on anything these days.'

Monsieur Pamplemousse, who had been listening with only half an ear, suddenly stopped in his tracks.

'Where did this happen, *Monsieur*? Here – in Paris?'

'Somewhere in the 8th *arrondissement*.'

'But you do not know exactly where?'

'Pamplemousse, I was in no fit state to take note of details, nor did I greatly care where we were. It was bad enough having to make a diversion in the first place. It was somewhere near the Parc Monceau, that is all I know. I remember glancing out of the window as we drove past the old toll house at the northern entrance and thinking not much further to go. What with all that and some wretched child crying incessantly I had a most unpleasant journey.'

'And you say you thought you had seen the nurse somewhere before?' persisted Monsieur Pamplemousse. 'Was it in the *hospice*?'

The Director shook his head. 'No. I have been through them all in my mind, one by one, and it was no one there. I think it must have been on the film set. She was very like one of the staff. I looked around at the showing but no one came to mind.'

Monsieur Pamplemousse fell silent for a moment. Something clicked in his mind. Reaching into his carrier bag he felt amongst folders filled with 20 cm × 25 cm glossy colour stills and several immaculately wrapped sample packs of soaps and perfume, until he came across what he was looking for. Removing an A4 size brochure, he flipped through it until he came across the picture he wanted.

'Was this the person, *Monsieur*?'

The Director stared at the photograph. 'You know I believe you could be right, Pamplemousse. She looked different in her working clothes, of course. And the girl in the ambulance had blonde hair . . . but I remember the green eyes . . . they were very distinctive.'

'*Merci, Monsieur.*'

Monsieur Pamplemousse felt a sudden surge of excitement.

The Director hesitated and then, realising he would get no further, abruptly changed the subject.

'I hope you had a happier journey back to Paris. You followed up my suggestions?'

'*Oui, Monsieur*. The restaurant you spoke of north of Orange was all you said it would be.'

'Remember also, Aristide, that it was not the truffle season. I must arrange for you to pay another visit now that October is here.'

'*Merci, Monsieur.*'

'And the *cuisine* at Pic?'

'As generous as ever.'

'That is good to hear. How about Bocuse?'

'He was there in person. He actually turned my *poulet* on its spit with his own hand.'

'A signal honour, Pamplemousse.'

'Poetry in motion, *Monsieur.*'

'I trust he did not . . .'

'*Non, Monsieur*. He did not realise I was from *Le Guide*. He simply happened to be going past. It was a purely reflex action.'

'I shall look forward to reading your report, Aristide.' Sensing a certain restlessness in his companion, the Director glanced at his watch. 'How time flies. It is nearly lunchtime already. I fear I have an appointment, otherwise . . .'

'I understand, *Monsieur*. But thank you.'

The Director glanced uneasily at Pommes Frites. Pommes Frites had been kept busy at the reception making his paw-mark on scraps of paper with the aid of an ink pad provided by a thoughtful PRO. There were still faint marks visible on the pavement where he had been walking.

'Can I give you both a lift to your car?'

'We walked, *Monsieur*. It was a lovely morning.'

'Walked? From Montmartre?' The Director coupled relief with a certain awe at the thought. 'I must say I envy your stamina, Pamplemousse.'

Monsieur Pamplemousse felt equally relieved as the Director climbed into his car and waved goodbye. He suddenly wanted to be alone with his thoughts.

Pommes Frites followed him across the Champs Elysées at the Rond Point. At the far end, beyond the Arc de Triomphe, clouds were beginning to roll in from the west. The sun which had been shining brightly not half an hour earlier now had a watery feel to it. Monsieur Pamplemousse gave an involuntary shiver. In less than two months' time the gardens surrounding the fountains on either side of him would be planted out with fir trees, all sprayed a seasonal white.

He could have kicked himself. Fancy not recognising the sound of Brother Angelo's bleeper that evening at the *hospice*. True, he'd had his mind on other things, but all the same . . .

He paused, as he always did, to admire the display in the window of the *chocolatier* a little way along the avenue Franklin D. Roosevelt. He would soon have to think about Christmas shopping. Doucette's favourites were the chocolate trees. He always bought her one as a 'surprise', although more often than not she couldn't bring herself to start on it until long after the holiday.

It took him exactly eighteen minutes to walk from the *chocolatier* to the Parc Monceau. He could have done it in fourteen, but Pommes Frites made several stops on the way.

Entering the park by the south gate, they encountered a stream of office workers heading in the opposite direction in search of lunch-time sustenance. A few of the hardier ones had already commandeered an empty bench and were tucking into sandwiches.

The joggers were out in force. Beds had been cleared of their summer plants and there were piles of newly swept leaves everywhere.

Through some gaps in the trees to his right he spotted the ubiquitous group of statuesque figures doing their Tai Chi exercises. A scattering of lovers braved the elements in sheltered nooks and corners.

Monsieur Pamplemousse picked an empty bench at a point near the centre of the park where the two main paths crossed. He settled himself down and began sorting through the contents of his bag, spreading the various items out on the bench in the hope that it might deter others from joining him. Pommes Frites stationed himself firmly at the other end of the bench, neatly obscuring a CHIENS INTERDITS sign.

All around the trees were changing colour. Behind him the *carrousel* was already covered for the winter, and the last few roses of summer looked as though they hadn't long to go.

Some children went past on tricycles. They were followed by a procession of *voitures d'enfant*, their occupants muffled against the autumnal weather. Heavily encased arms and legs stuck out at unlikely angles. If it were true to say that anyone who sat outside the Café de la Paix would eventually end up seeing the whole world go past, it certainly felt as though an afternoon spent sitting in the Parc Monceau must afford a glimpse of most of the children in the 8th *arrondissement*. It was simply a question of waiting, and Monsieur Pamplemousse had time at his disposal.

The press office had certainly gone to town. The brochure was a no-expense-spared work of art. The margins were as large as the bottles of XS were small.

There was a brief history of the company, with a run-down of all their successes. Failures, of which there had probably been many, didn't get a mention.

A rare photograph of Monsieur Parmentier headed an article on the subject of the science of perfume; mostly to do with the ingredients which had gone into the making of XS. Musk from the deer which roam the Atlas and Himalayan mountains. Ambergris from the intestines of whales. Civet from Asia, Africa and the East Indies. Cinnamon from Ceylon and Southern India for the American market. Other raw materials came from Egypt, India and Madagascar.

Von Strudel had a whole section to himself. There was a résumé of his credits over the years. It was an impressive list. Some films, like *The Babylon Years*, he remembered seeing as a young man; others he had to admit to never having seen, although they were still shown in art cinemas from time to time. Doubtless after the commercial appeared there would be a retrospective Strudel season at the Musée du Cinéma in the Palais de Chaillot.

He looked long and hard at the photograph of Anne-Marie, the key make-up artist. It would figure. According to the notes, she had worked on various pop videos and was credited with having suggested Brother Angelo for his role in the commercial. It must all have been planned a long time ago. Things were beginning to fit into place. Anyone wanting a change of personality would have expert advice permanently to hand.

Presumably it had been Anne-Marie who had visited the trailer that night. He wondered if she had any idea who the mysterious occupant of the bed was.

There were pen portraits of the others involved. The designer; the lighting cameraman; the sound supervisor; wardrobe; there was even a brief mention of Gilbert Beaseley.

Monsieur Pamplemousse closed his eyes, transporting

himself back in his thoughts to that first morning when he had met them all in the viewing theatre. And now Beaseley was dead. In his heart of hearts he knew he couldn't let the matter rest there. If he hadn't, albeit unwittingly, flushed Brother Angelo out of his hiding place Beaseley might still be alive. But was Ron Pickles capable of murder? By then he might well have been desperate enough. And had Beaseley been in the *Cathédrale* that morning, also hot on the trail of Brother Angelo? It would account for the telltale traces of white on his jacket. Perhaps he had left as soon as he realised Monsieur Pamplemousse was there too.

Brother Angelo must have engineered the flight to Paris with Anne-Marie long before the filming began. He would have needed someone who could transform his appearance; someone French who could cope with all the problems of getting him admitted to hospital and arranging for an ambulance to take him to Paris – no doubt there had been another suitable contribution to the *hospice* fund. Someone who could also arrange a place for them to go when they got there. Perhaps it was a case of being wise after the event, but thinking back there had been certain signs; something about the way they behaved together – the way Anne-Marie had removed the strand of hair from Brother Angelo's shoulder that day; not the automatic gesture of a professional at work, but of a lover. Now that he had a name and a face it was suddenly much easier to picture it all.

As for the various acts of sabotage, they were presumably made in an effort to delay the end of the production. It probably suited his purpose to make his flight to Paris when the city was as quiet as possible. There would be fewer questions asked. Changing the names round on the trailers must have been a precaution against being invaded by prying fans: a highly necessary one as things turned out.

It was late in the afternoon when Monsieur Pamplemousse felt a tug on Pommes Frites' leash. He let go of it immediately and Pommes Frites was away. Pricking up his ears, nose at the ready, he hastened towards a young girl with a pushchair.

Calling out in a way which he knew would have no effect whatsoever, Monsieur Pamplemousse followed on behind. As he drew near the girl he raised his hat.

'*Pardon, Mademoiselle.*'

He'd been half expecting it to be the Swedish *au pair*, but the girl spoke with an English accent. Again that figured. Ron would feel more at home with someone from his own country.

'Forgive me.'

'That's all right.' She seemed relieved to find someone who spoke her native tongue.

Never fully at ease with very small children, Monsieur Pamplemousse bent down to tickle the child's nose. It was hard to tell whether it was a boy or a girl, it was so protected against the elements.

'Fuck off!' Monsieur Pamplemousse jumped back as if he had been shot.

'That's very naughty. You know you mustn't say that.' The girl delivered a half-hearted smack on her charge. It had about as much chance of penetrating the thick clothing as a wet dish cloth.

'Oh, dear. I am sorry.' She blushed. 'She's a dear little thing really, but she just can't help herself. It's funny how children always pick up the worst. I shan't be sorry when she's had her operation.'

'There is something wrong?'

'She's going in next week to have some sort of bleeper thing fitted.' The girl looked round as though she was suddenly afraid of being overheard.

'Her father suffered from exactly the same thing and he had it done. She's lucky. Being bilingual could have been a problem, but they can programme it for more than one language now.'

177

'Coprophalia,' said Monsieur Pamplemousse, finding the word he had been searching for.

'Fancy you knowing that!' exclaimed the girl. 'I'd never heard of it before I got this job. I'm not sure I would have taken it if I had known. On the other hand, he couldn't be nicer and he thinks the world of his daughter. He sings to her every evening before she goes to bed.'

Monsieur Pamplemousse gazed down at the child. Dark, innocent-looking eyes gazed up at him. Her hair was a mass of black ringlets. Angelic was the word which immediately sprang to mind. He was tempted to reach down and give her another pat, but he thought better of it.

'Is she very like her father?'

'Not really. He's got fair hair. I don't know about the eyes – he always wears dark glasses.'

'And the mother?'

'I haven't met the real mother. They live apart. He never mentions her. But the woman he lives with is very nice. She used to be in films.'

'Would I know her name?'

'I doubt it. She was something on the technical side.'

Monsieur Pamplemousse was tempted to ask more, but already he was in danger of sounding over-inquisitive.

He raised his hat again. 'Forgive me, I am keeping you.'

'That's all right. We must be getting back home anyway. It was nice having someone to talk to.'

As the girl went on her way she turned to wave, then removed something from a basket at the back of the pushchair which she gave to the child. A moment later a small hand was raised. It was clutching a long, multi-coloured object which it began to wave in unison with the *au pair*.

Monsieur Pamplemousse stood transfixed, hardly able to believe his eyes. It was Exhibit 'A': the answer to all his questions.

178

For a split second he was tempted to run after them. Then he thought better of it.

Reaching down as though pretending to fondle Pommes Frites, he gently undid the strap on his collar, then he uttered a brief command. It was all that was needed.

Secure in the knowledge that Pommes Frites would not be back until the task of trailing his quarry to their destination had been satisfactorily completed, he returned to the bench to wait and to cogitate on what he had just seen.

'For *dîner*,' said Doucette, 'I have some ham from the Ardennes.'

'On the bone?'

'*Naturellement.*'

'Thickly sliced?'

'Just as you like it.'

Monsieur Pamplemousse heaved a sigh of contentment. Pommes Frites registered ten on his wagometer. It was good to be back home and in the warm.

'With it there is *purée de pommes de terre*, a little *salad verte* and some *salad de tomates*. After all your gourmandising this morning, and with Pommes Frites still being off lamb, I thought you might prefer something simple.'

'The simple things of life,' said Monsieur Pamplemousse, 'are often the best.'

'I have also opened that tin of olives you brought back from Les Baux. They look delicious.'

'Monsieur Arnaud is something of a perfectionist. I am told the black ones are kept in salt for at least three months – sometimes six until he is sure they are absolutely ready. The rest – the exact combination of herbs and sunflower oil – is a secret.'

'They look expensive,' said Madame Pamplemousse.

'You get what you pay for in this world, *Couscous*,' said Monsieur Pamplemousse.

As Doucette left the room he crossed to the hi-fi,

inserted a cassette, then picked up the day's *journal* and settled down in an armchair. Pommes Frites took up his favourite position – on the rug at his master's feet. Contentment reigned.

Perhaps that was why Brother Angelo had visited Fontvieille – not to see Daudet's windmill at all, but to buy some olives. Olives in Fontvieille; a Chinese meal in Les Saintes-Maries-de-la-Mer; a picnic in the Massif de La Sainte-Baume; sometimes it didn't pay to look for too deep a meaning in things.

Monsieur Pamplemousse glanced up from the *journal* as Doucette bustled back into the room carrying the olives in an open dish. 'I think, *Couscous*,' he said, 'we are shortly due for the Second Coming; a resurrection in the 8th *arrondissement*.'

'Really, Aristide,' said Madame Pamplemousse impatiently, 'you do come out with the strangest things at times.'

'Don't say I didn't warn you when it happens.'

It wouldn't perhaps merit a plaque, like the one in the Parc Monceau commemorating the landing of the first parachutist, but it would be a fitting end to all that had happened.

'What is that noise?' Madame Pamplemousse glanced towards the hifi.

Monsieur Pamplemousse held up the empty cassette case. 'It is the best of Brother Angelo.'

'If that's the best of Brother Angelo I would hate to hear the worst,' said Madame Pamplemousse. 'I don't know what the neighbours will think.' She turned down the volume. 'It doesn't sound like you at all.'

'I treated myself to it on the way home,' said Monsieur Pamplemousse. 'It is number one on the charts. The man in the store told me a whole lot of unreleased recordings have been found. Enough to keep the market going for several years.'

'It is a pity Brother Angelo won't be around to enjoy

the proceeds,' said Madame Pamplemousse.

'I am not entirely sure that is true.'

While his wife bustled around laying the table, he gave her a brief run-down on all that had happened during the day.

'But surely Brother Angelo already has another identity?' said Doucette in her down-to-earth fashion. 'Until all the fuss has died down can he not simply become plain Monsieur Pickles again? He has not really committed a crime.'

'Therein lies the problem,' said Monsieur Pamplemousse, 'I suspect that is just what he has done. He may not have meant to. It may simply have been an accident in the heat of the moment, but . . .'

'You don't mean you suspect him of being responsible for that man . . .'

'Monsieur Beaseley?'

'. . . Monsieur Beaseley's death? How can you be sure?'

'Something I saw less than an hour ago in the Parc Monceau.'

Doucette looked at him enquiringly.

'If you really wish to know, *Couscous*, it was a peacock's feather.'

'And that is enough to prove a man guilty of murder?'

'It could be more than enough. That will be for a jury to decide.'

Innocent or guilty? The outcome would depend on whether Brother Angelo was tried in France or in England. If it was the former he would have to prove his innocence. If it were the latter the authorities would have to prove his guilt.

'If there is one thing certain in this world, *Couscous*, it is that nothing is certain.

'I think possibly Monsieur Beaseley came upon Brother Angelo by accident. Perhaps he was hiding out up in a deserted part of the old town, waiting for nightfall. Or

Beaseley may even have followed him there. There was more to him than he let on and he was something of a nosy parker.

'If it was the latter, he may have confronted Brother Angelo. There was a struggle and in the course of it Beaseley fell to his death.

'That he was carrying a peacock's feather at the time I know, because he showed it to me before he said good-bye. It is extremely unlikely that Brother Angelo would have picked it up at the spot where Beaseley landed. The obvious alternative is that he picked it up after their argument and later gave it to his daughter.

'Did he fall, or was he pushed? Who knows?'

'What do you think, Aristide?'

'I think,' said Monsieur Pamplemousse, 'there are times when I am glad I am no longer in the *Sûreté*. It is for other people to reach such conclusions.'

Doucette opened the sample bottle of XS and smelled it. 'All that fuss for a tiny bottle of perfume.'

'The smaller the package,' said Monsieur Pample-mousse, 'the more expensive it is. Do you like it?'

'I am not sure it is you.'

'I am not sure,' said Monsieur Pamplemousse, 'that it is intended to be. It is altogether too complicated for my taste.

'I also think it is time I opened the wine and we have *dîner*. The ham will spoil if it is left too long.'

Pommes Frites pricked up his ears. As a 'nose' in his own right, he had decided views on the subject of smells. Had he been asked to venture an opinion he would have had to agree with his master; in the end the simple things in life were best.

When it came to scents, you could keep your XS. In his humble opinion there were few things to equal the aroma from a good *jambon*.

Had he been able to read Pommes Frites' thoughts, Monsieur Pamplemousse might also have put forward a strong case for the bottle of Beaune Clos des Ursules he was in the act of opening. It was from Louis Jadot and the bouquet reminded him of black cherries.

It would be a good marriage, the ham and the wine; a natural combination which rendered mere words redundant, like master and hound they simply went well together.